CAT'S CLAW

DOLORES HITCHENS (1907–1973) was a highly prolific mystery author who wrote under multiple pseudonyms and in a range of styles. A large number of her books were published under the D. B. Olsen moniker (under which her "Cat" series was originally published), but she is perhaps best remembered today for her later novel, *Fool's Gold*, published under her own name, which was adapted as *Band a part* by Jean-Luc Godard.

KATHERINE HALL PAGE's first novel, *The Body in the Belfrey* (1991), won the Agatha Award for best first novel. She won the award again for best novel in 2006 for *The Body in the Snowdrift*. Many more awards followed, including the 2016 Lifetime Achievement Award from Malice Domestic and culminating in being named Grand Master by the Mystery Writers of America in 2024.

CAT'S CLAW

DOLORES HITCHENS

Introduction by
KATHERINE HALL PAGE

AMERICAN MYSTERY CLASSICS

Penzler Publishers
New York

Published in 2025 by Penzler Publishers
58 Warren Street, New York, NY 10007
penzlerpublishers.com

Distributed by W. W. Norton

Cover image: Andy Ross
Cover design: Mauricio Diaz

Paperback ISBN 978-1-61316-626-0
Hardcover ISBN 978-1-61316-625-3

Library of Congress Control Number: 2024918730

Printed in the United States of America

9 8 7 6 5 4 3 2 1

INTRODUCTION

MISS RACHEL Murdock loves movies.

The septuagenarian sleuth in this novel by Dolores Hitchens, writing as D.B. Olsen, is keeping an eye on a "bandy-legged man," who in turn is keeping watch on the Sutter Street, Los Angeles, house next door. Miss Rachel immediately tells her ladylike older sister and reluctant Watson, Miss Jennifer, that Rachel would cast the "odd sort of man" as a cowboy: "A range cowboy who'd lost his mirror."

The films in Hollywood's Golden Age spanned the years 1930–1948 and America flocked to them. Miss Rachel thinks in cinematic terms and it's fun to view *Cat's Claw*, published in 1943, through that lens. When Miss Rachel experiences a feeling of dread she flashes back to "a remarkably good movie," *Hands of Darkness*, vividly picturing a moment when "a gorilla's paw slid through the curtain to hover over the innocent head of the heroine."

Cat's Claw draws on the horror movie genre that began in 1931 in the US with *Frankenstein* and Bela Lugosi and Boris Karloff's first appearance together in *The Black Cat*, a 1934 adaptation of Poe's short story. Hitchens may have been familiar with the short story as Poe's black cat, like the Murdock sisters' cat Samantha, contributes crucial plot devices. Samantha is an early feline sleuth. From 1939 to 1956, Hitchens published thirteen Rachel Murdock titles. She was a precursor to the trend of cat mysteries by cozy writers that began primarily in the late 1980s, notably by Lilian Jackson Braun, Carole Nelson Douglas, and Rita Mae Brown.

The other movie genre in these pages is of course the Western, given the case's locale: the San Cayetano Mountain, sixty miles south of Los Angeles. It's a very scenic backdrop, also called "Bear Heaven" because of the local belief that grizzlies still inhabit its summits. Dolores Hitchens personifies San Cayetano as rising from the Aldershot lands "with the abruptness of a humped monster." It's a terrain the author, who spent most of her life in Southern California, knew well. By page three, we have an abundance of cinematic ploys: "a million-legged horror" that awaits, "elements of murder," a widespread valuable property, and people in the case as memorable as the mountain itself. "I Can't Give You Anything but Love, Baby" is the soundtrack.

Although this imagined film would have been shot in black-and-white, Dolores Hitchens makes a point of describing the characters in color. Miss Rachel has a "snowy head" and Miss Jennifer's locks are "neat white ruffles." The two wear voluminous pale taffeta skirts over layers of starched white petticoats—"two little Dresden figures."

The dysfunctional Aldershot family is a version of *The Magnificent Ambersons* (1942). Robert is the oldest of the three children, suffering from a heart condition while wearing a costly "heavy purple robe and white silk pajamas." Harley at eighteen is the youngest with Monica in the middle. A Carole Lombard? Monica drives a blue coupé fast, has "sulky eyes," "lips painted frosty red," and a "haughty" demeanor. Her outfits, like the "ivory-colored sharkskin slacks," could have been designed by Edith Head. Spoiled rich girl Monica's bedroom ceiling is decorated in gold leaf.

The other femme fatale is Florence, first spied by the Murdock sisters in the Sutter Street backyard before she reappears in San Cayetano. She's slim with "sleek" dark hair and Miss Jennifer looks askance at her blue sun suit, but it's the tartan suit Florence later wears that's distinctive. The Aldershots have an uncle, Reuben Carder, living with them and he's in a wheelchair. An older man with a passion for avians and arachnids, he sports a "tiny mustache like a line drawn with chalk."

And there must be a romantic leading man. It's Tommy Hale, angrily working on the land his family once owned—a tall "dark young man" clad in denim.

Other characters play minor roles, including teen "brown-haired and freckled" Johnny—Mickey Rooney?—who drives a local delivery truck that Miss Rachel commandeers to investigate. He's a movie-lover as well and doesn't hesitate to join in the drama of a clandestine pre-dawn trip to the mountain's slate pit. LAPD's Lieutenant Mayhew makes a repeat appearance in this third Rachel Murdock book, his attempts to get her to stay out of the investigation fruitless. The cameras roll and the book's action, occurring over only a few days, is realistically compressed with a terror-filled roller coaster ride of an ending.

Cat's Claw is a variant of the "Had-I-But-Known" mystery, made famous by Mary Roberts Rinehart (1876–1958). If Miss Rachel had known what spying on the bandy-legged man and going to San Cayetano would have resulted in, her "appetite for adventure" would have taken her anyway. What the book does have in common with the foreshadowing type genre are teasers of what's to come starting on page two: "Tucked away in the ball of the future . . . were all the elements of murder, and personal, immediate, terrifying was the part she was to play in it." Hitchens often gives us Miss Rachel's thoughts in parentheses: "(How little she knew then!)" Others in italics: "*Or had it been . . . an accident at all?*" These asides, amuse-bouches, whet our appetites for what is to come and interject soupçons of suspense. Hitchens never lets them interrupt the plot. If some of the phrases are clichés in crime fiction now, they aren't here at an origin.

Cat's Claw is a fair-play mystery and Dolores Hitchens, while providing the clues, doesn't make the solution easy. It wasn't until a rereading that I spotted an early one that as a practitioner of the craft I should have noticed right away. She was a deft and ingenious writer with a gift for creating characters and striking descriptions of place that don't sound like a guidebook. Her sense of humor is obvious and despite the era, the book is not dated. From 1938 until her death in 1973, Julia Clara Catherine Maria Dolores Robins Norton Olsen Hitchens, to give her her full name, wrote prolifically, publishing as D.B. Olsen, Dolan Birkley, Noel Burke, and as Dolores Hitchens with her husband Bert—forty-six books and a play in total.

Why did Dolores Hitchens, who was in her early thirties and married, choose to write a mystery with a seventy-something sleuth and her sister, both spinsters? Was she inspired by some real-life Murdocks, deciding to make them visible, contradicting Miss Rachel's recollection about reading that "the elderly are almost invisible to the young"? Whatever the reason, Miss Rachel and Miss Jennifer were among a stellar company of spinster sleuths in the United States and Britain at this time. Surely a book on these indominable and independent women is overdue. Each would agree with Rachel's comeback after her sister speaks wistfully of "when we were girls": "I've had more fun since I've been older."

Miss Maud Silver, retired governess, opens a detective agency in London in *Grey Mask* (1928), the first in Patricia Wentworth's thirty-two book series. Sixtyish spinster sisters Amanda and Lutie Beagle move from upstate New York to take over their late brother's NYC detective agency in two books by Marjorie Torrey writing as Torrey Chanslor—*Our First Murder* (1941) and *Our Second Murder* (1942).

Stuart Palmer's former schoolteacher turned amateur sleuth, Hildegarde Withers, first appears in 1931. Hilda Adams would have been termed a spinster at age thirty in 1914 when Mary Roberts Rinehart's first Miss Pinkerton mystery was published. Her profession as a nurse provides Hilda with cover through four volumes.

Agatha Christie's Miss Marple appeared in 1930 and falls into the unmarried elderly amateur sleuth category as does Charlotte Murray Russell's Jane Amanda Edwards. Edwards is described as a "busy body spinster" training her eagle eye and wits on Rockford, Illinois, inhabitants in twenty cases from 1935–1953. Like the Murdocks and the Beagles, she has a sister, Annie, who shares Miss Jennifer's views on how a lady should behave. The amateur sleuths in this group have a convenient actual police detective to outsmart.

What all these women have in common is behaving against type. They may be "old maids" but they don't act like them. Miss Rachel and even timid Miss Jennifer think nothing of venturing up a twisting mountain path at ten o'clock at night to investigate in the dark.

Miss Jennifer, however, does balk at times, protesting her sister's "habit of expecting people to kill each other as soon as you

see them" and "dragging other people into trouble with them."
Miss Rachel is not overly "ruffed" since Jennifer has been saying the same kind of thing since she was seven and Rachel, age five, egged her sister into putting a frog in the church's collection basket.

Rachel Murdock may cause her sister some embarrassment, but she also expresses what all the other spinster sleuths represent in a variety of ways—the imperative to fight against evil. Rachel's words are classic: "There aren't any rules, any ethics, in murder . . . Do you think whoever killed him is carefully going over the moral aspects of the situation, crossing out things he mustn't do because they wouldn't be nice?"

The United States had entered the war by the time Dolores Hitchens was writing *Cat's Claw* but there is little mention of it in the book. Jennifer is knitting khaki yarn and there is war news on the radio. There's a scarcity of workers for the citrus groves. Johnny wants to be an aviation mechanic and see some action. That's about it. The big city, Los Angeles, now teeming with a massive immigration of wartime workers and cars adding to the already problematic smog, blackouts, and drills is worlds away.

In essence, *Cat's Claw* is a compelling mystery. Certain scenes and several characters linger long after the book is closed. Pour a finger or two of the Aldershot's good Scotch in a teacup as Miss Rachel does and sink into the long shadows cast by the craggy mountain.

—KATHERINE HALL PAGE

CHAPTER I

"I DO believe, Rachel," Miss Jennifer Murdock said severely, "that you have actually come down to spying upon people."

Miss Rachel drew in her snowy head from the outer side of the window shade; a pink blush stole into her cheeks. "It's only the bandy-legged man," she said. "He's watching them again. That same corner where the roses grow."

Miss Rachel was a little past seventy, calm and sweet, with skin as delicate as a camellia and hair like white silk. The only hint of her appetite for adventure lay in her eyes, which had the look of a child's at a surprise party. Life had not failed her in this respect, though it had been late in bringing her Lieutenant Mayhew and in revealing her knack for discovering what the lieutenant calls messes. Now she smoothed a pale taffeta skirt and watched Jennifer worriedly. "He's a very odd sort of man, Jennifer. So brown and uncombed-looking. If I were casting him——"

"Movies!" interjected Miss Jennifer with scorn.

"——I'd put him in as a cowboy. A range cowboy who'd lost his mirror." She went back to the other side of the shade.

"Our mother taught us," said Jennifer, "never to stare at

strangers. It isn't ladylike and it encourages rudeness in return. Now when we were girls———"

"I've had more fun since I've been older," Miss Rachel decided. "Besides, he keeps doing things that make one curious—like waving a handkerchief very quickly at that upstairs window and going out of sight behind those bushes when the young woman comes into the yard. I don't quite like it." She turned to stare at Jennifer, who was knitting. "I wonder what he's up to?"

Miss Jennifer held up a half-completed sweater in khaki yarn. It was beautifully knitted, but Miss Jennifer pursed her lips as if in displeasure. "I shouldn't wonder if it's something little and underhanded and rather cheap. Like bootlegging." Miss Jennifer had never quite got over Prohibition. "Or gambling—putting bets on race horses and that sort of thing. No wonder he doesn't want the wife to see him. The man in that house is no doubt very anxious that she shouldn't."

Miss Rachel looked down to where, on a lower level of their hill, a short man in very stiff, very new clothes stood staring at an upper window in the neighboring house. There was something eager and clumsy and half frightened in the gestures he made with his handkerchief.

"Gambling?" she murmured. It didn't look like it.

That was, Miss Rachel considered, the beginning of what she called "The Case of All Outdoors and Bear Heaven." It was then, when she first decided that the house below them on Sutter Street might be worth watching, that the ominous pattern began to unfold—a pattern comprised of many things of which she then knew nothing. Tucked away in the ball of the future, as securely as the rest of Jennifer's sweater into her ball of yarn, were all the elements of murder, and personal, immediate, terrifying was the part she was to play in it.

The million-legged horror that crept toward her in the dark while she waited, locked in and helpless, the slate pit with its ugly legend, the road that ended in a barricade, her first sight of San Cayetano: all of these waited in a cocoon of devious winding, whose end was to be found only with patience and the suppression of heart-knocking dread. Along the way were to be such minor horrors as the sheeted body on the kitchen floor, the stove that moved itself, and the thing that Jennifer found on the ceiling.

It was—though things began on Sutter Street in Los Angeles—essentially a rural drama, flavored with winy skies and the thrash of trees and long roads leading off into the distance. For backdrop it had San Cayetano, which rose out of the Aldershot lands with the abruptness of a humped monster: a blue bulk under the sun, a gray shape seen through rain, a solid blackness against the stars. San Cayetano, the mountain of moods, of wild beauties, of mystery and sadness; called by some Bear Heaven because of the belief that there still existed California grizzlies on its summits. San Cayetano—a mountain to remember.

And Miss Rachel remembered it. She could, in fact, never afterward forget it.

Not that the people in the case lacked any qualities to make them memorable—to think of San Cayetano was to think in the same instant of those who lived in its shadow: of Monica with her pale hair and sulky eyes, of Reuben Carder in his wheel chair, of young Harley with his youthful cynicism. To recall the Aldershot groves was to remember Tommy on the cultivator, jogging endless miles between rows of trees, staring past the oranges, as if not to see them was to forget what they had kept him from having. To remember the still evenings and the more silent nights was to recall the pathway through the orange trees, the thin shine of the stars, the breath out of darkness like the sigh of a giant.

The case was from its beginning an odd mixture of beauty and terror, and there were, too, its more comic aspects. Such as Jennifer with the mop hanging over her eyes, Jennifer's conviction about the rats, and the adventure of Miss Rachel's petticoats. Not that these leavened the terror—the terror that almost sent them running away.

Running wouldn't have helped. From the day that the bandy-legged man first lifted his handkerchief toward the upper window on Sutter Street the deaths at San Cayetano were as inevitable as the winds and the rains on Bear Heaven.

Miss Jennifer's first contribution to the case came in the form of a question at dinner. Over the chocolate pudding she looked thoughtfully at Rachel. "I wonder if he's there at night too?"

Miss Rachel had been so long at the window that she was stiff and sleepy; she had no difficulty in understanding to whom Miss Jennifer referred. "He was there when the last of twilight faded. He was sitting on the wall where the climbing roses are. He'd made him a little place, a sort of nest, and from the looks of it I got the impression he meant to stay all night."

"There aren't any horse races at night," Jennifer admitted. "Perhaps it's something else. He might be a bill collector."

"Bill collectors go home to dinner like everyone else. No. He's trying to see the man there without the woman knowing. I'm almost sure that's what he's trying to do."

Jennifer pounced. "A process server! Of course he wouldn't want the woman to see him. She'd warn her husband!"

"Hmmmm. No, Jennifer, he just isn't the type. Process servers are sly little men with glasses. Then people can't hit them."

"Where," said Miss Jennifer suspiciously, "did you learn all of that?"

"Well—I see things."

"Yes, Rachel, at the movies. I know. Your actual experience with process servers is just as broad as mine—which means it's non-existent." Miss Jennifer set her plain face in an expression of tolerant rebuke. "Please, Rachel, no fairy tales. The man's as apt to be a process server as anything. In fact, more likely, in view of his peculiar behavior." She paused to consider. "It's odd, though, that he waves his handkerchief. And the man in that house—I haven't noticed him outside for days."

Miss Rachel appeared revived by this show of interest on Jennifer's part. Dinner over, she led the way back to the living room and without turning on the lights she stepped across the floor and looked out at the window. "Come, Jennifer! You must see this!"

Miss Jennifer barked her skins on a footstool, grumbled at the dark, set the table in the window embrasure shaking. "Where? What is it? I don't see a thing; it's perfectly black and——"

The house below them, across the space of several vacant lots, was a lightless hulk under the faint gilding of a quarter moon. The roses made a thick hedge to separate the lawn from the embankment that let down to the street. In the thickest and most shadowy part of this growth there shone a pencil of light. Like an incredibly skinny finger it reached toward the house, crawled slowly up the wall as if exploring, settled on the pane, where the glass shone with an answering glitter.

"He's got himself a flashlight," Jennifer whispered as if the man might hear. "You know, Rachel, we might do best to call the police."

Miss Rachel was silent, waiting.

"He *could* be a burglar, waiting until they were gone to get in. Perhaps he's testing them now, trying to raise someone. . . ."

"Burglars don't come around in advance and wave handkerchiefs," Miss Rachel said. "Besides, it's *just that one room* he's interested in. He's acted very peculiarly for two days. If the street were full of houses he'd have been turned in by now. It's just that there's only us, and we're———"

"Look!" gasped Miss Jennifer. "Isn't that someone inside looking out?"

It did seem as though a white face swam in the gloom on the other side of the window and as though eyes—strangely hollow eyes—gleamed in the dim light. Miss Rachel held her breath, felt shivers go through her. Was the bandy-legged man to have his long vigil rewarded by a sign of life in the upper window?

Abruptly the shade came down and the pane was blank.

"Could it have been the man who lives there?" Miss Jennifer wondered. "Perhaps he's been ill. Did it seem to you, Rachel, as though the face were a bit—ah———?"

"Like a skeleton's? Yes." Miss Rachel kept her eye on the beam of light, which stabbed the pane with a series of flashes. "It's a queer business, Jennifer. How long is it, exactly, since we've seen the man out of doors?"

"I can't remember. It seems ages, come to think of it." Miss Jennifer's eyes grew bigger in the dark. "Rachel, it couldn't be another of your—your awful affairs, could it?"

Miss Rachel didn't look displeased; her profile against the night kept a shadowy sereneness. "If it is, it's much closer than any of the others. It shouldn't take long to get at the bottom of the business." (How little she knew then!)

"They couldn't be keeping him prisoner, or anything?"

"There's just his wife with him," Miss Rachel said. "At least I suppose she's his wife. They're alone there, and he kissed her one day out in the yard."

Miss Jennifer clucked doubtfully. "You can't be sure nowadays. Morals, you know." Her tone implied that morals were in a bad way. "Still, it isn't likely a lone woman could keep a man shut in if he wanted out."

"She's a very beautiful woman," Miss Rachel hinted.

"I never cared for that sleek kind of black hair, personally, and that blue sun suit she wears——"

"He's given it up," Miss Rachel said suddenly.

The light was gone, and the street below was a winding blackness under the faint moonglow. There was no sign of movement, of life, from the hedge of roses. Far at the bottom of the hill was an intersection and a street lamp. Miss Rachel kept her eyes on this, tried to catch any movement in the roses with the corners of her eyes, a trick she had found valuable. After a long while of waiting a figure detached itself from the other darkness, dropped to the sidewalk, and moved away. So poor was the light that Miss Rachel was not sure that she had actually seen it.

Then Jennifer whispered: "He's going away."

It was a strange end for a stranger vigil. Had the sight of the skeletonlike face been the answer for which the bandy-legged man had waited? Was his waiting over, his job done?

"I still don't like it, Jennifer. There's something wrong—twisted—hurtful——"

"No, Rachel. Don't go on about it. Let's turn on the lights and forget it. It wasn't anything. It interested us because we're elderly and alone and lead such quiet lives. At least I do," she added, remembering Miss Rachel's more lurid exploits. "You've gotten into a habit of expecting people to kill each other as soon as you see them." In this Miss Jennifer sounded vaguely like Lieutenant Mayhew. "Let's draw the shade and put on the lights and"—she shivered—"and let's put on the heat. I'm shaking."

Miss Rachel pulled the shade and pushed the light switch and even let Jennifer coax her into a game of dominoes, but her thoughts were elsewhere. They were with the bandy-legged man in a dark and windy street, trudging away; and the feeling came over her that the bandy-legged man had failed. He'd wanted more than the sight of a pale face swimming in gloom; there had been eagerness, a sort of entreaty to Fate, in his waving at the window.

What *had* he wanted?

"Rachel, don't sit dreaming. If you're tired we can go to bed," Miss Jennifer said. She yawned slightly to let Rachel know that she herself was not averse to retiring. "Let the cat out. I'll put these away." She began to stack dominoes into a box.

Miss Rachel went to the door, and Samantha, their black cat, followed. The front door opened on a high porch; steps went down to a little garden, an embankment grown over with geraniums. The street below was deep-cut like a river between vertical banks. From the height of the porch Miss Rachel could oversee the outskirts of Los Angeles, the lower windings of Sutter Street, the far-off intersection with its lonely light.

Mrs. Marble, their housekeeper, came into the hall on her way upstairs. Miss Rachel turned to answer her good night, and when she looked outside again she found her attention caught by the window at which the bandy-legged man had stared.

A blur of something pale floated where the drawn shade had

been. It was much too far to see details, but Miss Rachel's imagination painted in the enormous eyes which the flashlight had shown, the caverns under the cheekbones, the wasting of temples and throat.

The cat mewed softly, standing on the sill and watching her mistress. The tips of her fur and her eyes caught the light with a faint phosphorescence. She moved daintily out upon the porch and sniffed the wind. Miss Rachel followed, stared at the window in the other house, tried to make sure that the white blur *was* a face—even that it actually stayed there, remote and haunting. The shadows between mocked her efforts, distorted distances, played tricks with reality.

"That's the trouble," Miss Rachel told herself. "It's all shadow stuff, whispers, guesses. Jennifer and I have built up a fine fright—on nothing. There hasn't actually anything happened. Not anything."

She couldn't know, of course, how soon this condition was to be remedied.

CHAPTER II

THE RAPIDITY with which things happened in the early hours of the next morning more than justified Miss Rachel's apprehensions regarding the bandy-legged man.

The bandy-legged man was struck by a car.

That was the one thing of which Miss Rachel subsequently was sure. For the rest, the things for which Lieutenant Mayhew prodded her memory in vain, she had no answers. The make of car, its color, its license number—even part of its number—its driver, its direction when it turned at the bottom of the hill: these things Miss Rachel admitted sorrowfully that she didn't know.

The bandy-legged man had come back very early to his post under the wall beside the roses. He looked, Miss Rachel thought, a great deal tireder and more discouraged. He didn't wave his handkerchief; he simply kept out of sight and watched. And somehow, looking down at him from the height of her bedroom window, Miss Rachel felt sorry for him. He was, subtlely, like a well-trained dog that keeps a forgotten post when its master is gone.

Miss Rachel and Miss Jennifer had breakfast, and Mrs. Marble, their housekeeper, served her opinion on the bandy-legged man along with the toast. "I'd turn him in for loitering if I were you. 'Tisn't right to go skulking about the way he's doing. Make him explain himself, that's what I'd do."

Long afterward, when circumstances had "explained" the bandy-legged man and the depths of his tenacity, Miss Rachel regretted that she had not followed this sensible advice.

She said a little worriedly: "I'll keep an eye on him and see if he means any harm."

She had scarcely gone to the living-room window when it happened. With an air of suddenly giving up, of going finally away, the bandy-legged man had left the shelter of the wall and was crossing the street with a slow, awkward stride. His head was down, and there was a stupefied air about him, as if the loss of sleep and the suspense had begun to tell on him. He was at about the center of the pavement when a car lurched into sight, a long car moving soundlessly and giving no warning.

Miss Rachel screamed, forgetting the bandy-legged man couldn't hear her. In the instant before he was caught and thrown he looked up. There was no time for any expression to cross his face. The car had swung down from the top of the hill, and he had been walking at a slight diagonal, with his back half toward it. The car struck; he rose awkwardly, his arms flying, the shape of him like a broken kite spiraling to earth.

The car slowed with a horrible screaming of brakes; for an instant Miss Rachel thought that it meant to run over him. Then it crept close to the sprawled body; a humped dark figure got out on the side opposite Miss Rachel and engaged in some movement she could not see.

Miss Rachel stood rooted, amazed and hopeful. "They're taking him to the hospital," she said aloud. "I wonder how badly he's hurt? I wonder"—her eyes went to the blank, curtained panes of the house below—"I wonder if *they've* seen him?"

The body of the bandy-legged man was slowly vanishing into the car as into the maw of a monster. Some feeling of unease, of mistrust in her interpretation of the thing, decided Miss Rachel against staying at the window. She ran to the front door, tugged for a moment because it stuck, stepped out upon the front porch, and looked down. The car had taken up its silent progress. The thought that the motor was off struck Miss Rachel; for some time she failed to connect it with the fact that the bandy-legged man hadn't looked up until the last instant. Now she watched, a little puzzled and nonplused, as the long car stole down the hill and vanished into the distance.

There didn't seem to be anything to do.

It was a strange ending for the vigil of the bandy-legged man, but for a while Miss Rachel was inclined to take it on its face value: an accident, the victim rushed off to help in the car that had run him down.

But the thought of it nagged her during the rest of the forenoon. She found herself looking at the closed blinds of the house below theirs. Since the vigilant waiting of the bandy-legged man had been for some purpose in connection with that other house, it seemed strange that no notice had been taken of his accident.

Or had it been—Miss Rachel shivered—*an accident at all?*

A vivid remembrance of that last instant when the man looked up to see the rushing car came back to her. He hadn't made any sudden move; he hadn't seemed horrified or overcome by his impending fate. He'd just—*stared.*

Yes, he had stared, she recalled, as if he were trying to see something so well that he should never forget it.

She went restlessly to the window when luncheon was over.

Miss Jennifer was knitting. She had accepted Miss Rachel's story of the accident with an odd look of concern; Miss Rachel thought that Jennifer was a little disappointed that their mystery had ended so abruptly.

Below, the space of vacant lots was yellow with dried grasses, and the house beyond looked shrouded and sullen under lead-colored autumn skies. "I wish," Miss Rachel murmured, "that I'd thought to take the number of that car."

Miss Jennifer looked at her intently over her knitting. "Yes, it's odd that you didn't. You were a witness, and people aren't always honest in reporting a thing like that. The driver may have said that the man was to blame."

"It was almost as if"—Miss Rachel paused—"as if the driver *meant to run over him.*"

Miss Jennifer sniffed loudly in the silence. "Don't you think you might make a few inquiries?" she said. "Just to be sure he's been taken care of properly? I don't mean for you to get involved, Rachel, or to push yourself into that queer business of watching the other house. But you might ask. You might ask Lieutenant Mayhew and let him find out for you."

Miss Rachel spent a minute thinking over what she should say to the lieutenant. Mayhew had always had a distinct aversion to what he called Miss Rachel's "messes." He would, she thought, consider the oddity of the bandy-legged man's vigil a sort of mess. Not a major annoyance such as she had brought him before, but definitely irritating. Miss Rachel decided to tell Mayhew about the accident alone; it was the sort of thing he could get his official teeth into and not an evasive quality like the other.

She called Mayhew at police headquarters, and he left his study of microscopic enlargements of a human hair to answer.

His voice was masculine and comforting. He would, he promised, look into the matter of the accident. It would have been reported by now, naturally.

Miss Rachel went away from the telephone feeling very much reassured. The bandy-legged man, whatever his motive in his spying, was in good hands now. Official routine would take care of him.

An hour later Mayhew called back. He wanted the license number of the car. Miss Rachel couldn't give it. He wanted, then, the color and make of the car and a description of its driver. She hadn't that, either. Suppose, then, she give him an exact description of the victim.

She did this in detail, and Mayhew's scribbling came back over the wire in an erratic whisper.

"Haven't you found him?" she asked.

"Not yet." Mayhew was always noncommittal. "I'll call you later. No, wait." She waited, visualizing his brown face full of thought, his steel-colored eyes intent and measuring. "I'll be out there shortly, and you can show me just where it happened. I'm coming by on another errand, and I'll stop."

Miss Rachel is familiar with the lieutenant's peculiarly uninterrupted and direct style of driving. She spent the intervening minutes getting into a coat and reassuring Jennifer's fretful worry lest she annoy the lieutenant with the vagueness of the bandy-legged man's behavior.

When she opened the door and found Mayhew there, big and brown and very official, she asked him in. He declined with thanks, saying that he had urgent business elsewhere. He'd just take a look at the spot where the man was hit. He followed Miss Rachel down the steps, through the garden, and by way of a cement ramp to the street.

Miss Rachel paused. It was a little difficult, from here, to determine just where the man had been walking when he was struck. The perspective had changed. Miss Rachel decided to stay on the walk until she reached the place where he had started to cross the street.

She asked about Mrs. Mayhew, who was her good friend, and in listening to Mayhew's answer she neglected to look closely at the neighboring house when they passed it. She had an impression of closed blinds, of general desolateness, but a detail which was to become important later escaped her. At the spot under the wall where the bandy-legged man had waited, sheltered by climbing rosebushes, she struck off on as near a duplicate of his path as she remembered.

At about the center of the street she paused and looked involuntarily behind her. The street went direct to the top of the hill, climbing steeply between vacant terraces once it passed Miss Rachel's house. At the very top, against the lead-colored sky, the snout of a car made a stubby irregularity in the outline of the hill. Miss Rachel drew a sharp breath and waited, but the car was not moving; it was parked. She felt impatient at her own nervousness. She'd be seeing ghosts next.

Mayhew was prowling the pavement near her, his eyes cast down to pick out anything of interest.

"In what direction was he thrown?" he asked.

"Downhill and toward the other curb." Miss Rachel cast another glance at the half-visible car above; she couldn't help it. "I think he may have struck the other curb, though I'm not sure. It all happened very quickly."

"The fact that the accident hasn't been reported might not mean anything crooked," Mayhew said with an air of thinking aloud. "It could be that the man wasn't seriously hurt and chose not to be treated. In that case the driver might not think a report was necessary—though it is, of course." He walked slowly toward the other side of the street. "Or, even if he were hurt slightly, he might not want his presence here in this neighborhood known. We had a case like that not long ago; a man was keeping a girl in an apartment and didn't want his wife to know about it. He gave a false name at the time of the accident and left before the doctors could examine him fully. He died that night of a skull fracture."

"I suppose people have all sorts of reasons for trying to fool the police," Miss Rachel said, remembering the peculiarity of the bandy-legged man's long watch. "But wouldn't a skull fracture have killed him right away instead of later?"

"Not necessarily," Mayhew answered, still strolling. "I'm no doctor, of course, but I understand there are several types of—types of fractures that——" His words died away, and he stopped and stood perfectly still. In the silence Miss Rachel was conscious of the sudden far-off roar of a motor, but she failed to look toward the top of the hill. She was watching Mayhew.

He had knelt, his big body cumbersome inside his heavy overcoat, and was staring with bent head at a spot on the curb just beside a small ragged bush. With a careful touch he lifted the fringe of its branches. Miss Rachel went toward him, and he glanced up to motion her away. She pretended that she hadn't seen him. After all, the bandy-legged man was hers after a fashion, and she had the right to know what had happened to him.

"Very well," Mayhew said with an air of giving up. "Here's where he struck. The bush concealed it from the street." With a suspicious look he tugged at the bush, and it rolled easily toward him. "Moved, obviously." His glance settled a few feet away.

"There's the stub where it grew. The driver of the car must have acted quickly. I don't like the looks of this. Nor of these." He picked up four white objects and held them out in the palm of his hand.

Miss Rachel saw with a little shiver of sickness that the four white objects were teeth.

"And here's part of his scalp." Mayhew's finger indicated a smudged, red, sticky place on the curbing. "There are hairs stuck in it and bits of flesh. He's had a serious head injury; he's knocked out four teeth—probably when the car hit him—and it's been some hours since he should have been reported and taken care of." Mayhew glanced at his wrist watch. "We'll have to get on this right away. I'll use your telephone. Wait here for me, will you? Just in case."

Mayhew didn't say just in case of what, but Miss Rachel looked at the top of the hill where the car had sat with its nose pointed down at them. It was gone. The grassy terraces rose to the sky, and the street was empty. A little wind passed up the hill, blowing Mayhew's overcoat against his knees and undulating the grasses like the motion of water. Miss Rachel shivered again and decided that after all she had better tell Mayhew the rest of it: the story of the bandy-legged man's watch from under the rosebushes.

She tried to find some sign of motion, of life, in the house across the street. It was a drab house and had been rented furnished for some years to a succession of tenants. Mrs. Marble had usually managed to find out a few details about the current occupants and pass them on to Miss Rachel and Miss Jennifer. But of these last tenants Miss Rachel remembered no single bit of gossip. They had kept to themselves, the young man and his wife, and were in a less spectacular way as much a mystery as the bandy-legged man himself.

She frowned at the closed blinds of the upper story with their hint of secrecy and inner darkness. She wished she were bold enough to go to the door with a pretense of making a neighborly call. How easily, she thought, a really bold, nosy woman could get at the bottom of all of it, and she imagined herself with a nerve of iron walking up the path to the door.

Mayhew appeared then on her own porch, and over the shoulder of his descending figure Jennifer's face looked down. Miss Rachel had no need to be told what Jennifer was thinking, the warning her eyes meant to convey.

"I can't help it," Miss Rachel said miserably to herself. "It might be very important, after all." As soon as Mayhew had joined her she told him of the thing the bandy-legged man had been doing.

He listened, his brown face fixed in a masklike repose that betrayed none of his thoughts. When she had quite finished with all the details he swung and looked at the house and then began to walk rapidly toward it.

"If they ever saw him, they gave no sign," she said, hurrying to keep up. "He was there two days. The only sort of answer they gave was to pull down the blind when he shone his flashlight on it."

"The man here," Mayhew flung back. "You say he's disappeared?"

"Only into the house, apparently," she answered. "We both thought it looked rather like him—the face at the window—except that it was terribly wasted, as if he'd been ill."

They were on the walk. Mayhew stopped abruptly, and Miss

Rachel almost ran into him. She peered past to see what it was that held him stock-still and watchful. The windows—there was nothing at any of them; the old panes gave back the dull light blankly.

Then she saw. It was the door, standing open, swinging a little with the press of the wind.

CHAPTER III

THERE WAS no electric button at the door but simply a knocker. Mayhew used it resoundingly. The echo of it went back into the old house as a pebble into the depths of a well, and they waited, Mayhew and Miss Rachel, looking at each other thoughtfully. Then Mayhew called in through the door, asking if there was anyone at home, and again there was the impression of lifeless vacuity swallowing the sound.

He pushed the door wide and strode in, Miss Rachel following, and they were in a hall. Steps went up inside an old-fashioned carved banister at their left. Ahead and to their right was the lower floor of the house. Mayhew went through the rooms quickly. They were furnished with large ancient pieces, a great many red drapes and oil paintings. Miss Rachel got the impression it might have been furnished as a fashionable home in about 1915. The stuff had stood up under renting because it had been stout to start with. Now it was nicked, dusty, glazeless.

The upper floor, where two bedrooms faced the street and one the rear yard, yielded something of interest. The absence of personal belongings was at once noticeable in these more intimate parts of the house. Mayhew ran through drawers, closets, wall cabinets.

"They've cleared out." He slammed the last door shut. "When was the last you saw them?"

"Last night," Miss Rachel said slowly.

"No sign of them this morning?"

"No." They were in the bedroom whose windows the bandy-legged man had watched. Miss Rachel stared at the wall absently where the water-color painting of a mountain hung opposite the high-postered bed. "Perhaps he knew it—knew that they were gone, I mean. Perhaps that's why he seemed suddenly to give up, to lose hope." She wrinkled a usually serene forehead. "He *did* seem hopeless this morning. He looked—defeated, walking away."

Mayhew was looking down into the street. "Well, I'm going to leave you and start things moving at headquarters. I'll put a man in this house. Who handles the renting of it, by the way?"

Miss Rachel gave him the name of the local agent, who was known to her.

"They've cleared things pretty thoroughly," Mayhew said in going downstairs, "but I believe I'll have a look at what they've left for the trash collectors."

In the barrel beside the rear fence they discovered old newspapers and a great many medicine bottles.

"Looks as though someone's been sick, right enough." Mayhew stacked the bottles neatly outside the barrel. The papers he rummaged through, then thrust back into the container. "There are several bottles with prescription numbers on them. That might lead us somewhere." He thrust the few bottles with druggists' labels on them into the pockets of his coat. "Now. Let's go up and I'll use your telephone."

They went back to her house, and Miss Rachel listened while Mayhew set in motion all the elaborate machinery of a big city's facilities for crime detection. She closed the door after him as he hurried away and watched when his car roared up the hill and vanished over the summit. Then she removed her wraps and joined Jennifer in the living room. Jennifer was winding a new ball of yarn, and the cat had a lazy eye on the tantalizing thread.

It was very peaceable and quiet.

Miss Rachel sat down and then stood up. Miss Jennifer raised her brows and wound the wool a trifle crookedly. "Now, Rachel," she said.

"He's taken it away," Miss Rachel said.

"*It?*" echoed Miss Jennifer, though she must know.

Miss Rachel nodded without explaining.

"Why do you always regard these—ah"—Miss Jennifer almost used the lieutenant's word, "messes," and then decided it wasn't very ladylike—"these unfortunate crimes as your own personal property, Rachel? They are strictly the business of the police. Of course Mr. Mayhew has taken it away—I presume by *it* you refer to the mystery he will very shortly clear up. You should *want* him to take it away. You've done your little part in calling it to his attention. Now let him work it out in his capacity as a detective." She gave Miss Rachel a suddenly stern eye. "An *official* detective, Rachel."

The black cat rolled over in a sudden excess of mischief, seized Miss Jennifer's yarn, and snarled it in her paws, and then sprang up and raced away like a shadow.

"Oh, whatever possessed her?" cried Miss Jennifer, mourning. "At her age. You'd think she was a kitten."

Miss Rachel looked with interest at the tangle that the cat had made and then walked to the window and stared through it at the autumn sky.

"Now what?" Miss Jennifer asked uneasily.

"I'm just thinking," Miss Rachel said.

Before lunch the house below was being thoroughly gone through by the police. Nor was the curb with its ominous stain being neglected.

Miss Rachel ate a superb cheese soufflé without comment— to Mrs. Marble's secret grief—and under Jennifer's uneasy eye she kept silent, her face withdrawn and thoughtful. She was ticking off to herself the things the police would be doing: fingerprints first, of course; then hair combings, the height of things on the shelves, the quality and selection of the stock of groceries left behind, a hundred and one things to complete the picture of the vanished tenants. All of it minutely scrutinized, noted, catalogued. And past reach of her knowing, as though the whole thing were taking place on Mars.

Mayhew, when he came back briefly, had nothing to say, and this was his grave error. Miss Rachel is not by nature unco-operative. But Mayhew's determination that she shall not dabble in police business is a spur to rebellion.

"Could I," she asked innocently when he stood on the porch, ready to go, "just have a look through the house once more?"

He started to answer, and she broke in with: "I'm familiar with the furnishings, you know." This was the baldest of lies, and Miss Jennifer stopped knitting to stare. "I might—I just might notice something worth while, and I could tell your man."

"I see. Something changed or missing. Very well, you might try it. I'll speak to Edson on my way." His brown back disappeared down the ramp to the street. Miss Jennifer made *tisking* noises at the sweater in khaki yarn.

The cat came back to lie in the sun. "You aren't fooling me," Miss Jennifer said severely. She looked at Rachel, who found it convenient not to hear.

At three o'clock Miss Rachel returned with several articles in her arms. They were things which Edson had given her permission to study. She put them down on the little table before the davenport: a sheet of newspaper, the water-color painting of a mountain, a shred of bright woolen cloth in plaid.

Miss Jennifer glanced at them quickly and then concentrated on her knitting.

"I——" Miss Rachel stopped; this was going to be very hard to say. "I think I'll go away for a bit, Jennifer."

"Where?" cried Miss Jennifer.

"To the place those people came from. The couple in the house. The bandy-legged man too, perhaps."

"But you don't know where they came from!"

"I'm pretty sure that I do."

Miss Jennifer looked apprehensively at her sister. "The rental agent? Did he tell you?"

"No. I saw him at the house, but he knows nothing of the couple who lived there. He was glad, he says, to be able to rent the place without asking any questions. It's run down, you know. The name they gave was Smith. That seems to show lack of imagination and not much else. He hasn't any idea of where they came from or where they went. They gave no notice. He came over because the police had been asking questions on the telephone."

"Well, then, if——"

"They paid their rent by two-week periods, which might mean they wanted to be ready to leave on short notice. He was never in the house during their occupancy and doesn't know what sort of stuff they had with them. Except——" She tapped the water-color painting of a mountain, a blue craggy bulk above a valley in green. "This must have been theirs because he hadn't ever seen it before."

Miss Jennifer leaned over her knitting to peer at the little picture in its plain wooden frame. "That? But I don't see——"

"It's not a professional piece of work. Even I can see that. It looks—somehow—as if someone painted it who loved the scene, who wanted to put a bit of it down and have it for his own."

"That's imagining things," Miss Jennifer put in.

"I know. I do. I can't help it. The picture was on the wall opposite the bed where the sick man may have lain. You see, it may have represented something very dear to him, and that's why he had it where he could see it constantly."

"But, Rachel, please. You can't go hunting mountains."

"There is a name lettered in the corner," Miss Rachel went on. "*San Cayetano. R. A. 1940.*"

Miss Jennifer grew a little pale. The knitting needles faltered. "I don't enjoy being left alone," she said miserably.

"Jennifer, please don't start worrying now. Look. I have other evidence. I went through their discarded newspapers; they were all recent, all of last week's, except this one page. It had been saved from more than a month before. And here"—she held the slightly yellowed sheet where Miss Jennifer could see it—"here's an article that ties in with the picture."

Miss Jennifer read the headline as if unwillingly.

CITRUS GROWERS OF SAN CAYETANO PROTEST
PRICE LEVELS

San Cayetano, Calif., Aug. 30, 1942.—Citrus men of this locality have petitioned the national association for a review of price levels to be arranged with the help of government agencies. With the orange harvest shortly to be picked, and workers scarce, the growers feel that an upward adjustment of prices would help solve the labor shortage. This is expected to be . . .

Miss Jennifer shut her eyes suddenly, and then a tear squeezed through her lashes. "Rachel—just this once—don't try to do it yourself. This horrible thing happening to the man in the street may not have been an accident. The lieutenant's beginning to think it wasn't, I'm sure. Let the police have it. Don't go away and meddle with this trouble."

Miss Rachel watched the slow progress of two tears down Miss Jennifer's sallow cheeks. Of the two, Miss Jennifer had always been the plain one, the unsprightly, the sensible low-heeled, bun-on-the-neck type. She wasn't given to demonstrations of emotion, and so the tears must mean that during Miss Rachel's previous absences she had been very lonely indeed. The excitement gradually ebbed out of Miss Rachel, and for once in her life she looked a little gray.

"If it means so much to you, Jennifer——"

Jennifer's eyes came open slowly. "Would you, Rachel, just this once? I'd appreciate it more than I could ever say. If you'd give Lieutenant Mayhew these things you've found—it's wonderful, really, how you've reasoned it out—and let him follow them up and tell you about it later, I'd be so happy."

Miss Rachel smiled a trifle weakly and put the folded news-paper upon the picture and the scrap of wool between. "Very well. When he comes I'll give him these."

Miss Jennifer gave her a keen glance. "And you won't be so awfully unhappy, will you? Won't it be rather a relief to have Mayhew do it all, have the risk, the hardship?"

"He'll be under a handicap, of course," Miss Rachel said slow-ly. "He can't go out of his territory. He can't go quietly up to San Cayetano as we could have done and nose about and get the background of the thing. There must be a background."

Miss Jennifer got her breath suddenly. "As *we* could have done? But, Rachel, I wouldn't dabble in such things. I wouldn't touch them."

"You don't know, until you've tried, just how fascinating it is to work on a case like this," Miss Rachel explained. "Look at the information we have already. We know that a couple who called themselves Smith rented an isolated, furnished house and paid their rent only two weeks ahead. They were there about—just how long were they in that house?"

"More than two months," Miss Jennifer said after some thought. "I remember the day they moved in; Mrs. Marble and I were taking down the curtains upstairs. That was about the mid-dle of July, when we bought the new pink ones for the bedrooms. I saw them come in a taxi. They had four suitcases, and on one suitcase was strapped a large board like an old-fashioned bread-board, only thinner."

"A drawing board," Miss Rachel said. "Of course. He or the girl does water colors."

"We were hanging and ironing curtains most of the day," Miss Jennifer went on, warming to her subject, "and I noticed them in the yard. I was at the windows, you see, and they were right below. The girl had taken off her jacket and had on her plaid skirt, and she picked a few flowers. . . . By the way, didn't you have a bit of plaid cloth there?"

Miss Rachel drew the scrap of woolen cloth from beneath the page of newspaper. "Yes, it was behind a dresser. I suppose it fell there. It looks as though it had been cut off as a swatch, a piece to compare with. Do you know, Jennifer, it's an authentic old Scottish plaid. I don't know of what clan, offhand, but I remember a pattern like it from that book on the history of weaving I had last week from the library."

"They're copied everywhere, I suppose," Miss Jennifer put in. "It wouldn't necessarily mean anything."

"No. And yet you saw her wearing a plaid suit, and she'd scarcely cut a piece out of it for comparison."

"It may simply have taken her fancy."

"Some of the Scottish families cling to such things, especially if their line is pure and they come from a royal clan. Remember the MacDonalds we met on our trip East?"

Miss Jennifer took the piece of cloth away from Rachel and smoothed it over the back of her hand. "It's very pretty and fine wool too. I suppose you could look it up. Out of curiosity, of course."

"Of course," Miss Rachel agreed. "As I was saying, the things we already know——" She went on about the bandy-legged man, the long silent car, the flight of the couple whose name, at least temporarily, had been Smith.

Miss Jennifer listened between fascination and terror. She did not, during the afternoon, press Miss Rachel about getting hold of Lieutenant Mayhew. She had silent spells during which she appeared to think of something rather frightening; at dinner she spilled the tea.

In the small hours of the night Miss Rachel awoke to the sound of movement in Jennifer's room. She crossed the hall in her nightdress and put an eye to Jennifer's door, which stood ajar. Jennifer's bed had not been slept in. There were on its smooth counterpane two objects: the black cat and an open suitcase. Jennifer was talking to one and putting clothes into the other.

"She'll be the death of me yet," Jennifer said. "I shudder to think what might be waiting for us in that place."

The cat moved and stretched and cast an oblique shadow on the wall.

CHAPTER IV

THE MISSES Murdock, two small and elderly ladies, stood in the one street of the village of San Cayetano and looked northward. In the distance, against a background of peaks farther and more vague, rose a blue craggy monster whose outline was familiar. "It's an impressive sort of mountain," Miss Jennifer whispered. "You wouldn't forget it easily."

Miss Rachel studied the far-off heights with their hint of wooded gully and blue crevasse. "There isn't any mistaking it," she said. "The surprising thing is that whoever painted that picture caught so much of its—its flavor." She seemed dissatisfied with the inadequate word. "Its personality—if a mountain has one."

"There's something about it———" Miss Jennifer let her eyes drift from the long rising terraces of orange groves to the abrupt jutting roughness of the mountain, like something upheaved from below. "I suppose we might walk up that way. Or is it too far?"

"Let's ask Mrs. Simpson."

Mrs. Simpson was an acquisition of that morning. She was the hostess of the one establishment in San Cayetano which took in wayfarers, the proprietress of a huge old home whose rooms she rented out—when there were renters. She was gray, placid, stout, and she, like the little village, showed no infection of the giddiness of Los Angeles just sixty miles away.

Miss Rachel and Miss Jennifer found her studying a seed catalogue in the parlor. "The mountain?" She glanced at them in surprise. "It's pretty far for you to walk. You can't realize, I know, how far it is. It looks near because it's so big." She must have seen their disappointment. "I'll tell you what—the grocery sends a delivery truck up that way this afternoon. I'll speak to Johnny if you'd like."

There were things Miss Jennifer just would not do. She frosted the landlady with a glance and began: "I'm afraid——"

"Of course." It was Miss Rachel's appreciative voice. "Will you ask him? We'll promise not to be any trouble at all."

Mrs. Simpson looked a little puzzled. "It isn't a bad truck; it's almost new, and the seat's closed in. I think you'd be as comfortable as though you were in an ordinary car. You'd see the Aldershot place when Johnny goes there. It's just at the foot of San Cayetano and it's beautiful."

Miss Jennifer remained cool over the proposal of riding in a delivery truck, but in their room Miss Rachel was full of enthusiasm. "He may even know who those people were. I'll find a way to describe them to him, very casually, of course. Would you begin with the bandy-legged man?" She frowned at the bonnet she was preparing to put on. "Or with the girl? The girl, I think. A boy who drives a delivery truck ought to know of every pretty girl in the country."

"And they may have been a couple just passing through, just stopping long enough to paint the mountain, and be long gone, long past his remembrance." Miss Jennifer's tiredness from the bus trip was taking the form of pessimism. "All that you had was the picture, Rachel. Don't build too much on that."

"The newspaper article," she reminded. "It was all about a labor shortage in the orange groves. Would a passing artist keep it? I don't think so."

Miss Jennifer sighed. "I don't quite feel up to a ride in a truck, Rachel." There was more than a hint that she was beginning to regret coming. "Would you mind awfully if I didn't go?"

So it was Miss Rachel went alone. Johnny proved to be about eighteen, brown-haired and freckled, and as movie-conscious as she was. They compared notes on current films. From the cab of Johnny's little truck Miss Rachel looked ahead to a long road lined with eucalyptus trees, the roof of a big house, red tile and white stucco chimneys, a slow rise that ended on the flank of San Cayetano.

"All of this," Johnny said after a slight lapse in the conversation, "is Aldershot land. My dad knew old man Aldershot. He's dead now. I guess the Aldershots're about the most important folks around here. Richest, anyhow."

"Do they own all the land between here and the mountain?"

"Every inch, and the mountain too." Johnny pointed to the faraway roof whose chimneys shone in the yellow sunlight. "That's their new place. My sis says that Monica Aldershot's room has a little pattern around the edge of the ceiling in real gold leaf. You'll get to see the outside of the house and the grounds. The uncle, Mr. Carder, goes in for peacocks and pigeons—other stuff, too, not so pleasant, though I've never seen anything queer. You'll notice the birds. They're everywhere."

The heights of San Cayetano, craggy against the pale sky, held Miss Rachel's fascinated attention. She only half heard Johnny's remarks about the Aldershots, though they were to come back later with an increment of terror and loathing. She was watching the angled slash up the side of the mountain. "Could one walk up a way, do you think? There seems to be a road."

"The road to Bear Heaven? Yes, I suppose you could walk it if you'd like. I'd get permission first; it's Aldershot land—not that they'd care. They've got so many miles of brush and timber up there I don't suppose they even know where it ends."

They were leaving the main road now, entering a driveway in gravel where long streamers from pepper and eucalyptus trees drifted to make shadow over them. The white house was set in lawn; it was of Spanish architecture: recessed in doorway and window, low of roof, grilled with a lacework of iron wherever possible. It looked to Miss Rachel a trifle overdone, a little too heavy, too ornate. Three peacocks wandered on the lawn, turned startled eyes on the car as it swung in, greeted Johnny with harsh cries of alarm.

"If you do go up," Johnny was saying, "try to see the slate pit. I'll tell you the story about it sometime. The slate, you see—— You can't get out." He broke off; they were behind the house now, at the rear where a wide cement porch faced a graveled courtyard and stables, pens, and vast bird cages in which fluttered pigeons and doves.

Miss Rachel stepped out as Johnny vanished into the kitchen with a box of groceries. She wondered if this might be the point from which the water-color picture had been painted. Above, in the still light, San Cayetano shut out the sky; its flanks were furry with brush, and cows a little way up looked down placidly on the Aldershot groves. This was too close, she thought. The picture had had greater depth, perspective, and there had been no detail of the mountainside, just blue bulk and remoteness.

She heard the purr of another car from the front drive and

looked back. A blue sedan had stopped, and a stout man got out carrying a small satchel. He nodded to her briefly and walked out of sight toward the door. At the same moment there was a crunch of gravel from behind; Miss Rachel turned to meet the stare of a man in a wheel chair.

Pigeons clung to the arms and the back of the chair, and their fluttering cast a fantasy of shadow on his gray-white hair, his heavy eyes, his long face with its tiny mustache like a line drawn with chalk.

"Is there something I can do for you?" He touched the wheel, and the chair twisted a little so that he had a fuller view of her. "Were you looking for someone?"

"No, thanks. I—I came riding with the delivery boy from the village."

"Oh." He took his eyes off her and looked hard at the other car, the sedan. "I thought you might have come with Dr. Pete. Just seeing the sights, are you?"

"We're staying with Mrs. Simpson—my sister and I. Jennifer didn't feel like riding, but I thought as long as I was here I might as well see some of the country."

"San Cayetano? I noticed you looking at it. There are quite a few legends about it, you know."

"I don't believe I've heard any."

"Oh, the slate-pit story." He looked at her again, and she saw that his eyes were a clear expressionless green, and she knew, somehow, that when he had been young he had been a strikingly handsome man. "Then the story about the grizzlies. I can't quite believe that one, but it's just possible that it's true. There's supposed to be an Indian burial ground. . . ." His voice drifted down, and Miss Rachel had the impression that he was testing her, that in some obscure way he was searching her mind for curiosity, interest, avidity that he might pounce upon. She kept still.

"Am I boring you? No? I thought you might have heard some of those old legends in your stay here."

Miss Rachel almost said that she had only arrived at the village that morning and then did not. "I was interested in it because it's so beautiful," she answered. "I thought I might walk the road a way sometime soon, if I could get permission."

"Do you sketch or paint?" he asked indifferently.

Miss Rachel said that she did not.

"It is my nephew's hobby. He, too, is fond of San Cayetano, though he is not engaged in painting it now." There was some irony behind the words, and she felt his concealed but close attention; at the same time, Miss Rachel's heart literally rose into her throat to choke her.

"I should think San Cayetano might tempt even an amateur," she said, and wondered if her tone betrayed her.

"It has tempted many." He had, she saw, a way of putting enigmatical meanings into simple words. "In many ways."

Some chill off San Cayetano's shadowy summit drifted over her; she found the light green eyes studying her carefully. The well-modulated voice said: "It grows cool early this time of year."

At that moment a girl came out upon the cement porch and looked at the man in the wheel chair. "Dr. Pete wants you, Uncle Reuben. He's got to go back; he'll meet you out in front." Her glance settled on Miss Rachel. "Hello! Was there something I might do for you?"

She was a tall girl with pale curling hair, a wide mouth painted a frosty red, and sulky eyes the color of the man's. "I'm Miss Aldershot," she explained.

"I just came riding to see the mountain."

Monica Aldershot's eyes went from Miss Rachel's little taffeta figure to the sleek delivery truck. "With Johnny? Oh, I see. How do you like San Cayetano up close?"

Uncle Reuben was twisting past her; he threw Miss Rachel a look of sly humor. "You've gotten Monica started. I leave you to her." He rode away, the pigeons fluttering after.

Monica laughed carelessly. "Uncle Reuben doesn't like San Cayetano; he's fond of saying that it's kept the sunlight off the Aldershots for fifty years. Makes us sound moldy, doesn't it?"

Monica was so perfectly beautiful that Miss Rachel couldn't keep her eyes off her. "I'm sure that none of you are the least moldy. And I do like your mountain. It dominates the valley like a giant. We noticed it, my sister and I, from the village, and Mrs. Simpson arranged this ride for me."

"Mrs. Simpson is nice. You don't get a good view here from the house, though. Our tenant house in the grove has a better one. Ask Johnny to stop there for a minute on the way back. The place is vacant. Don't hesitate about going there."

"Someday, if I might, I'd like to walk the road a little and see what the valley looks like from up there." She indicated with a nod the yellow line that etched the flank of the mountain. "If you'd give me permission."

"Of course." Monica's attention was caught at that moment by the man carrying the satchel—Dr. Pete, Miss Rachel presumed—and her uncle, together at the door of the sedan. "Sometime soon when I'm in the mood we'll drive up." The hint of arrogance in the words was belied by the friendliness of the glance she gave Miss Rachel. "It's lovely. It's like having wings. I'd better go now and hear what Dr. Pete has to say. I'll see you again before long."

The casual promise was not one in which Miss Rachel put much faith. She was trying to pin into her memory the things Reuben Carder had said about his nephew: that his hobby was painting and sketching, that he wasn't doing it now. Could that mean illness? Coincidental with the presence of the doctor, it might very well mean just that: that here the trail ended, that the sick man from the house in Los Angeles lay inside the Aldershot home.

Johnny came out, brisk and humming, and he and Miss Rachel drove away. Past the front of the house where Monica Aldershot waved to them briefly—she stood with an arm on the back of her uncle's wheel chair—past the lawn with its peacocks, down the long lane with its trailing greenery. Johnny burst into song.

Miss Rachel hesitated to ask him to stop at the tenant house. Johnny was a busy young man, and the delay might be an annoyance to him. She decided to ask directions and to walk out in the morning. She spent the time on the ride back with casual questions about the local people: had any of them moved away recently or come home again? (This under the guise of comments about the movement of population in regard to war industries.) Who was talented? Who painted, sketched, wrote? Had she heard correctly the man in the stage depot (here a description of the bandy-legged man) saying he was from San Cayetano, or did such a person live here?

The results were mixed. The wealthy landowners came and went constantly, leaving their groves to trusted overseers. The village people stayed put. The workers, the cultivating hands and the pickers, came in seasonal waves like the tide and left on its ebb. Right now the citrus men were having an awful time getting help. It was Johnny's opinion the landowners might have to get along with a few less limousines and pay their workers better. War was war.

Painting, sketching, and writing were things of which Johnny was aware because people did them in the movies. In San Cayetano? He wouldn't know. His girl liked to paint old furniture in freakish colors. Was that art?

The bandy-legged man reminded Johnny of old Tim Woodley. His brother Jeff worked for the Aldershots; old Tim did, too, before he got his leg broken falling out of a fig tree. Funny about old Tim—hadn't seen him around lately; maybe he'd gone to visit their sister in Victorville. That would account for Miss Rachel's having seen him in a bus depot.

Johnny himself expected to be traveling shortly. He was going to be an aviation mechanic and help have a lick at the Japs.

Miss Rachel found Miss Jennifer fretful. Samantha was under the bed and wouldn't come out. There was no hot water in the tap. Dinner was late, and Miss Jennifer was hungry.

Investigating these griefs, Miss Rachel found that Samantha had discovered herself a mousehole and was not to be budged; her green eyes looked fury at Miss Rachel's timid interruption. The tap gave warm water if you let it run long enough. Dinner? She'd ask Mrs. Simpson what time it would be.

Dinner would be at seven.

At seven they walked into Mrs. Simpson's dining room, where the white napery, the shining silver and glass, the hint of heavenly food from the direction of the kitchen made them feel as though they were royalty.

The feeling went away when they saw who was waiting for them. Across the table, slim and dark-haired and still wearing the plaid suit, sat the girl who had called herself Mrs. Smith.

CHAPTER V

Miss Rachel felt at once swelled with pride and punctured with humiliation. Her methods of reasoning things out had been justified. But she had been caught. The girl would know them. She would know them for the sly, spying little old spinsters they were (at least in Miss Rachel's confused conscience). She would be quite angry and she would be within her rights in denouncing them, right at the dinner table.

All of this while Miss Rachel was advancing toward the table with the girl's cool, introspective gaze upon her. Miss Jennifer was hanging back; her breath was hoarse in Miss Rachel's ear.

Mrs. Simpson swept in with a tureen of soup. "Oh, there you are. You haven't met Miss MacConnell, have you? Miss MacConnell, these are the new ladies I spoke about, Miss Rachel and Miss Jennifer Murdock. Now we can all sit down and be friendly." She laughed in her placid way. "It isn't often I get to introduce anybody. Folks just know each other around here."

The girl nodded. Miss Rachel found herself sliding into a chair. She was getting oriented to the idea of eating with the ex-Mrs. Smith.

"What on earth brought you ladies to this out-of-the way hole?" the girl asked in an ordinary tone.

"My health," Jennifer croaked. This was Jennifer's line; they'd prepared the answer in Los Angeles. "My health required a change."

Jennifer sounded, indeed, as though she were dying, to Miss Rachel's ears, but this might aid the illusion. The girl gave her a sympathetic glance and murmured a conventional solicitation.

"Nothing like the air at San Cayetano," said Mrs. Simpson, dishing up the soup. "You'll snap right out of it. It's better than Arizona, if I do say so myself."

This implied disease wasn't quite the one they'd planned for Jennifer, but Miss Rachel let it pass. She was thinking furiously. There had been no inkling of recognition in the girl's behavior. Miss Rachel remembered having read somewhere that the elderly are almost invisible to the young: so many gray figures passing on the outskirts of their vivid and lively world. Could it be that in Los Angeles Miss MacConnell had noticed the Misses Murdock so slightly that she didn't recognize them now?

It was, Miss Rachel decided, highly probable.

And the girl's being here . . . Miss Rachel trembled a little with nervous pride. It was the answer to all of Jennifer's doubt and Lieutenant Mayhew's brusqueness. The picture of the mountain and the clipping from the paper had been valuable and valid clues. Even the meaning of the scrap of plaid had been correct. Miss MacConnell was Scottish, and there was in her speech the slightest trace of a burr.

"How did you happen to hear of San Cayetano?" the girl asked Miss Jennifer curiously.

"Oh, we just started out, and this looked very attractive." Miss

Jennifer took refuge in helping herself to salad. "I need the quiet too."

"Do you know," Mrs. Simpson said, "we have so very little sickness in San Cayetano that I believe I could name on the fingers of one hand all whom I know who've been ill this past year? There's Mrs. Maltry's rheumatism, but it really doesn't count; she will not quit making that dandelion wine, and that's what's doing it. Then there's the eldest of the Aldershot boys, Robert. He's developed heart trouble, and they say he's very bad."

The girl had stopped eating and was looking blankly into her plate.

Mrs. Simpson looked at her. "Not meaning to remind you of anything unpleasant, Florence. We all feel that your father was treated very unfairly."

There was no answer from Florence MacConnell. She did, after a moment, raise her eyes and look directly at Miss Rachel. "You don't understand," she said quietly. "But go on with what you were saying."

Mrs. Simpson continued with the illnesses of local residents. Florence had lost her appetite. Miss Rachel plotted feverishly how she might get Mrs. Simpson away and pump her without the placid lady's knowing. Miss Jennifer alone did justice to the dinner, eating in a manner wholly at variance with the supposed state of her health. Jennifer seemed to have the idea that if she kept chewing no one would ask her questions. Oddly enough, it worked.

When dinner was done Miss MacConnell went to her room, and she was scarcely out of sight before Mrs. Simpson clucked distressfully and said, "Poor child! Such a time she's had."

Miss Rachel and Miss Jennifer were at the archway that led

into the living room. Mrs. Simpson was stacking dishes for the maid. "Mr. MacConnell—that's her father—worked for the Aldershots for over fifteen years. There's just him and Florence, and he was such a good father to her. Mother, too, for that matter." Mrs. Simpson drew a big breath and let it out on a sigh. "We all liked them so well, and he worked so hard for his little girl. None of us could understand how such stories got around. I never believed any of them, not even when he was fired and made to move out of the tenant house."

Miss Rachel stood absolutely still and didn't by so much as an audible breath interrupt the flow of information from Mrs. Simpson.

"Some say he was caught drunk, lying on some hay in the barn and smoking. The Aldershots have some wonderful horses, and it would have been serious—but I didn't believe it. Then there's a story that he had a slight argument with Mr. Krug, the manager of the ranch, and in revenge put emery dust into the tractor motors. I don't believe that either. There's just one of the stories that might be true. . . ." She paused; there had been a peal from the front-door bell. "Excuse me." She hurried past into the hall.

Miss Rachel followed Miss Jennifer, who had gone into the living room and sat down with a magazine. From the hall came the rattle of the lock, the slow creak of the door's opening. "Oh!" said Mrs. Simpson. "Well, Mr. Krug!"

This, Miss Rachel remembered, would be the manager of the Aldershot property. She decided he might be worth looking at and walked casually out, as though on the way to the stairs.

Mr. Krug stood in the open doorway with the gray light of early evening behind him. He made a spry, thin, grasshoppery silhouette, but because of the gloom Miss Rachel failed to get the details of his features, and amazement overcame her at what the two of them were saying.

"I thought I saw a certain young lady in your yard today, Mrs. Simpson." His voice was dry and deep and authoritative. "I don't mean to pry; I just wanted to make sure. Is Miss MacConnell here?"

"Indeed not, Mr. Krug. You've made a mistake." Mrs. Simpson's silhouette was immobile and big, and her arm made a bar across the doorway that kept Mr. Krug from coming in.

"We hold nothing against the young woman, you understand. But if she's come back—— Perhaps she needs help; perhaps Mr. MacConnell has had trouble getting work elsewhere——"

"If Miss MacConnell were here, she wouldn't wish your help, Mr. Krug."

"Just to talk to her——" He made a peering motion; Miss Rachel wondered if he could see her in the depths of the gloomy hall. Perhaps the living-room light showed her, too, as a silhouette. "Miss MacConnell?" he asked loudly in Miss Rachel's direction.

"Good night, Mr. Krug," said Mrs. Simpson, shutting the door firmly in his face. "Go tell your Mr. Carder," she said angrily to the closed door, "that your spying and sneaking won't do him any good."

A soft mutter filled the night from the other side of the valley. Miss Rachel remembered that she had seen, from the cab of Johnny's truck, a series of low hills and the spindling derricks of oil wells in that direction. Standing now at the window of the room she shared with Miss Jennifer, she looked out at stars, a quarter moon, the floor of the valley in darkness, and a twinkle of lights where the derricks would be. The sound of their motor-driven pumps varied as the wind changed; the flowered curtains lifted and sagged, and there was the smell of night-blooming jasmine.

"I'm ready," Miss Jennifer announced. She had drawn a chair to the little bedside table and was sitting in it, a pencil poised above a sheet of writing paper. "You think and I'll write it down. We should draw up a summary and a plan of things to be done. Let's begin with the situation in Los Angeles. We had a man and a girl living there under assumed names. Could they actually be married, perhaps, Rachel? I hate to think——"

"We aren't primarily concerned with their morals," Miss Rachel reminded, "though we can, when the time comes, let Lieutenant Mayhew find out if their marriage is registered in any local county office." She came to sit on the bed near Miss Jennifer. "I'm afraid Lieutenant Mayhew will be very cross this time. He'll feel that I've meddled in something that belongs strictly to him. I wonder how he's come out in the search for the bandy-legged man."

"If he's been found alive there isn't much point in our being here," Jennifer pointed out.

Miss Rachel glanced at the little clock on the dresser. "We must go down at ten o'clock and hear the news on the radio. That may give us something. Well, to go on—this couple was living there, and there was an attempt made to contact the man. Remember, Jennifer, how the bandy-legged man always hid when the girl came into sight? It was Robert Aldershot he wanted. He didn't get hold of him because Mr. Aldershot was either too ill to get up and investigate or else was avoiding him. Let's put down those two possibilities."

"Aren't you presuming a bit in being sure that it was Robert Aldershot?" Miss Jennifer asked.

Miss Rachel reached to where Samantha slept on the counterpane and stroked a black ear which twitched in answer. "Not a great deal. The girl's being here is one clue to his presence; her reaction to Mrs. Simpson's mention of his illness was another. The initials on the painting were *R. A.* He lives at the foot of the mountain in the picture; he paints as a hobby. No, I think we may safely assume that Robert Aldershot is Mr. Smith. The one we still must identify is the bandy-legged man."

Miss Jennifer wrote rapidly in an angular, old-fashioned hand. "Johnny thought he might be Tim Woodley who used to work for the Aldershots. Tim's brother still works for them. Put down item one in things to do: find some way to meet Jeff Woodley and ask him about his brother."

"Would we dare try to question Miss MacConnell?"

"We couldn't possibly do it without arousing her suspicions and giving ourselves away."

"No, I suppose we couldn't."

It was at that moment that there was a rap at the door, and Mrs. Simpson came in with a pitcher of fresh water and two glasses on a tin tray painted with forget-me-nots. "Are you ladies comfortable? Not too chilly? Light the gas if you feel you need it."

She bustled about, inspecting the supply of towels and blankets. Since she had turned Mr. Krug away she had had this air of being extremely busy. Miss Rachel thought that she was a little embarrassed at being overheard lying to him. "Well, all set for tonight?" she asked at last.

"We were wondering," Miss Rachel said, "if we might listen to the ten o'clock news broadcast."

"Certainly. Feel free to use the radio at any time. You won't disturb anyone. The bedrooms are all far enough so that the sound won't carry." She hurried out with a brief good night.

It was a quarter of ten. Miss Jennifer put away the sheet of paper in her suitcase, and they went down to a darkened and deserted living room. The gas log burned with a faint sputter. The cat walked about, exploring the unfamiliar place, mewing hopefully at the door from the dining room into the kitchen. Miss Rachel lit a single globe in a floor lamp and looked up to meet Miss Jennifer's forlorn gaze. A train whistle sounded far away.

"I wish we'd stayed home," Miss Jennifer whispered.

Miss Rachel was engrossed in getting the radio started. It came gradually to life with a hum; voices spattered through; then the sign-off of the commercial announcement came and the news began.

There were war and politics and rationing, a digression into sports, a nip back into history for comparison with similar events of more than twenty years before. And then, incredibly, there it was in their ears: the horror that concerned the bandy-legged man. He was found. He was dead: mangled, butchered, and buried hastily in the dry bed of the Los Angeles River where it wandered cross country between Compton and Long Beach. He'd been dug up by a hunter's dog, identified by means of missing teeth and other wounds as a man who had been acting peculiarly in an outlying neighborhood in Los Angeles. There was no other immediate means of identification. Persons having information concerning him—here his description followed—should get in touch with Lieutenant Stephen Mayhew of the Los Angeles police. Furthermore, the whereabouts of a couple living at a certain address (the one next Miss Rachel and Miss Jennifer on Sutter Street) and who had left suddenly was desired.

"And us. He'll be looking for us," Miss Jennifer moaned, bug-eyed. "You know he's missed us. He'd have wanted us to look at—at *it*."

It was so quiet then—Miss Rachel had snapped off the radio—that the ticking of a clock in the dining room was like the knocking of a heart.

"I've just thought of something," Miss Rachel said slowly.

"Going home?"

"Of course not. The car. The car that hit the bandy-legged man. I saw it. If I could see it again, if it's a car belonging to someone here——"

Miss Jennifer's teeth chattered.

"I should have found some way to look into the Aldershot garages."

"But, Rachel, why on earth would any of them——?"

"The bandy-legged man went from here to Los Angeles. Whatever it was he had to see Mr. Aldershot about must have been important, and it must have been secret. Someone in a big luxurious car killed him to prevent that meeting. I thing the Aldershot garages are the first on our list, obviously. Have we our new flashlight with us, Jennifer?"

Miss Jennifer choked.

"We could be there before midnight. There's a slim possibility that there might even yet be time to discover something. The murderer may not know——" She paused.

There had been an audible click from the hall.

Miss Jennifer looked over her shoulder and shivered. "What was it?"

Miss Rachel went out very quickly and flicked on the hall-light switch. The hall was empty. So were the stairs, the upper landing, the closet under the stairs, and all of the rooms on the lower floor.

Miss Jennifer made the significant discovery. Their tour of inspection over, they were again in the living room, and she was staring at the floor. "Samantha!" she said suddenly. "She's disappeared!"

They made the tour again: hall, closet, pantry, dining room, kitchen, service porch, and found no trace of the cat. But a querulous mewing had begun to reach them from somewhere near. High and frustrated, it led them back again into the hall, to the door, to the wide front porch.

Samantha showed a fuzzy back and eyes spitting rage under the porch light. She was outside. Only the passing of someone through the front door could have put her there.

CHAPTER VI

"It's so dark!" Miss Jennifer complained. "I've turned my ankles on this gravel a dozen times!"

"Keep off the gravel," Miss Rachel cautioned. "Walk behind me here on the grass. There's the house. See it?"

"We've been long enough getting here!"

"To the left of the house is the driveway. I was only as far as the back door, but I'm sure it continues to garages—somewhere. Listen! What was that noise?"

"Ducks, Rachel. They'll give us away. You know how a duck is; he never sleeps; he——"

"Shhhh!" Miss Rachel pulled Miss Jennifer after her into the shadow of an oleander tree, where the pale taffeta of their dresses would not glimmer in the darkness and betray them. "Somebody's coming. Listen!"

It was then, in her awkward hurry, that Miss Jennifer by accident snapped on the flashlight. A yellow beam sprang out, struck the foliage on the opposite side of the driveway, showed them Samantha sitting there watching with round green eyes.

"Jennifer!" cried Miss Rachel. "Turn it off!"

"I c-c-can't!" Miss Jennifer chattered. She was working madly with the switch; the yellow beam made circles on the drive, and the cat watched them interestedly.

"Hide it somehow!" cried Miss Rachel.

The beam abruptly went off, and there was no sound whatever from Miss Jennifer. Miss Rachel put out a hand where Miss Jennifer had stood, found emptiness, felt fear shoot through her.

"Jennifer!"

"I'm sitting on it," Jennifer said miserably. "Rachel, did you see? Samantha's followed us, and we thought we'd shut her in tightly."

"We did shut her in." Miss Rachel paused, and the slow crunch of approaching footsteps was clear. "Someone's been out through Mrs. Simpson's front door, as they were while we were in the living room. There's something peculiar going on in that house. I don't like it."

"We're acting as peculiarly as anyone could——"

A figure, a darker splotch in the gloom under the trees, came down the driveway and would have passed them, but the cat mewed.

"No!" moaned Miss Jennifer under her breath. Another flashlight had come to life and searched for the cat in erratic circles.

"Kitty? Kitty?" coaxed a voice—Monica Aldershot's voice. Miss Rachel shrank back and held her breath, remembering Monica's friendliness and the fact that they were trespassers—dark-of-the-night trespassers. "Here, kitty! Why, you're black. No wonder I couldn't see you. *Kitty?*"

Samantha looked up with eyes of green flame and mewed an answer, and Monica's slim white hand came into the light and stroked the black satin head.

"What are you doing here? Out tomcatting, I suppose, like

the rest of the male animals." There was a hint of irony here. "Or are you on the lookout for baby pigeons? Mustn't, if you are."

Miss Jennifer made a slight choking sound, but whether of fear or at the idea of the respectable and aged Samantha being a tomcat, Miss Rachel was not sure.

"Why don't you," said a new voice out of the dark, "give the cat a chance to speak for himself?"

Monica's hand stayed quiet for an instant—too quiet; it looked like marble—and then she straightened up and said, "Well, another visitor?"

"Surprised?" said the voice. It was a clipped, lazy voice with a teasing overtone, and it must have annoyed Monica Aldershot, for she suddenly swung the flashlight full on the speaker.

He was a dark young man in working clothes. His hair was curly, cut short; his eyes mocked her, and the scrubbed skin of his face and throat shone in the yellow light. "Or were you out looking for me?"

"Obviously not." Her tone was freezing. "I would like to know what you're doing here. Not working so late, certainly."

A red flush stole into his skin, but he continued to look into the light with a steady stare. "Not working," he agreed. "This comes under the heading of boredom, sightseeing, or whatever you want to call it. I'm just looking around."

"You'll hardly see much at midnight."

"I've seen you."

The flashlight dropped off him suddenly and then went out. There was a moment of silence so intense that Miss Rachel's ears hummed with it. She could see the shape of the house up ahead, a dim bulk in white, and San Cayetano like a black hole in the sky. But the people in the driveway were shadows—voiceless shadows without movement or reality.

Monica's voice came again, quietly. "Tommy, don't you ever get tired of sparring?"

"Not especially, darling. You taught me, you know. I was a fool, and you were my hank of hair—or whatever it was Mr. Kipling gave fools for their downfall. Now I faw down. Boom!"

There was a sound as though he were laughing, but Miss Rachel couldn't be sure. Without the ironic young face to speak it, the speech sounded a little sad. She wondered why a boy in working clothes should have played the fool to haughty Monica.

"Tommy, I've forgotten all of those things you said that day. About M-Miss Money-bags, and Uncle Reuben——"

"Has Uncle Reuben forgotten? Has he forgotten my remarks on his spider collection? I'll bet he hasn't!"

There was silence, as though Monica might be thinking out her answer. "You mustn't be too harsh in your opinion of him. He's tied down to his chair, and he gets bored and tired. If you'd handled him right, if you'd gone at things differently——"

"He'd have still said what he did. You're very rich, Monica. You own umpteen thousands of acres of rich orange lands. You even own San Cayetano—my dad sold it to your dad, so I ought to know. You own cows, barns, nice automobiles, and furs. Yes, and you even own a bedroom trimmed in gold leaf. The village can't get over it. Uncle Reuben couldn't get over the idea of a hired hand aspiring to all of that. He never would get over it. Imagine Mr. Thomas Hale coming in off the tractor and climbing into bed under a ceiling of gold leaf." He laughed, real laughter this time, young laughter full of a desire to hurt.

"Don't be vulgar, Tommy."

"Vulgar? No, I don't have to be that, do I?" The laughter had stopped. "I can kiss your hand, madame. You'll wash the hand afterward, politely in private, of course. I can bow the knee and tug the forelock. Someday"—his voice was like a hammer, beating out its words upon the offended silence of the girl in front of him—"someday I'll have money, Monica. There'll be a way—*there has to be a way*. And if you make the mistake of marrying me then, my lady, I'll take great pleasure in seeing you live in hell."

He swung with a crunch of gravel, and Monica's flashlight came on instantly and focused upon his back.

"If you ever come near the house again," Monica's voice said, following him, "I'll have you horsewhipped."

He looked back, and though his face was white and his mouth worked, his eyes still mocked her. "Be sure it's a pedigreed horse-whip."

The light went out, and the sound of the young man's foot-steps died away. The wind made a soft rustle in the trees. Above in a black sky the stars shone glassily. It was growing cold. Monica Aldershot stood where she had stood when she had talked to Tommy Hale. Miss Rachel could hear Jennifer's heavy breath-ing; she wished she could see what Monica was doing.

Suddenly Monica said, "Good kitty. Are you still here?" And after another minute or so she went back toward the house.

Miss Jennifer whispered, "Do you think she's crying?"

Miss Rachel didn't answer. She was shivering, looking at the dim house and the vast darkness of the mountain. Monica, shad-owy and slim, went in at the door; no lights came on inside the house.

"He was crude, wasn't he?" Miss Jennifer said.

"He's very determined to hurt her," Miss Rachel answered. "Sometimes people with that obsession will go to any length to carry out their ideas. I wonder—did you catch the remark about money?"

"Her money? Yes, that irked him."

"No. The money he means to have. He let that slip because he was angry. Now. That flashlight, Jennifer."

Miss Jennifer rose, and they worked together with the catch. It was quite thoroughly stuck. They ended by taking the flashlight apart and removing the battery.

"We'll have to do it in the dark, then."

"Not another step, Rachel!"

"It isn't far. The garages must be just the other side of the house."

"Did you hear the other thing—the awful thing—that young man mentioned? *A spider collection?*"

"Hmmmm. That explains Johnny's remark," Miss Rachel said thoughtfully. "What an unpleasant man this Mr. Carder must be."

"The point is, Rachel, I am not—*I am definitely not*—going to snoop about any property with a spider collection on it."

"What on earth harm could a dead spider do you?"

"He didn't say a word about their being dead," Miss Jennifer proclaimed. "Big, hairy, crawling things. Ugh!"

Miss Rachel knew that the accident with the flashlight and Jennifer's terror of spiders had defeated her. And yet—to have been so near, to have made the long walk successfully, only to have her plans ruined because of a cat and a stubborn switch. She sighed; then her eyes widened. A light had come on at the far side of the Aldershot house.

The window was out of sight around the corner, but there was a yellow square against the shrubbery, a reflected glow that shone on gable and tile and ironwork.

"Come on!" she urged.

"Not spying!" gasped Miss Jennifer. "Rachel, you wouldn't!"

"You've already said that I would."

"I know, but—but looking *in* at windows——"

"Is no worse than looking out of them. It's murder, Jennifer. Can't you understand that? There aren't any rules, any ethics, in murder. The bandy-legged man was run down and taken away and slaughtered. Do you think whoever killed him is carefully going over the moral aspects of the situation, crossing out things he mustn't do because they wouldn't be nice?"

Miss Jennifer resisted, but Miss Rachel pulled her across the driveway and up the lawn to the side of the house where the light shone. Neat, tiny, they were like two delicate little mice creeping up on a delectable bit of cheese. By standing on tiptoe they could see into the room.

Monica Aldershot was there, just inside the door. She was dressed—now that they saw her in the light—in ivory-colored sharkskin slacks with pockets and neckline trimmed elaborately in blue braid. She still carried the flashlight. Under the pale hair in its froth of curls her face was stormy.

Dimly through the pane they heard her say: "You've got to let him go; tell Krug you want him discharged. I won't go on like this. He's making a fool of me."

A man propped up with pillows in the middle of a big bed took his hand away from his eyes and looked at Monica. He was thin; his eyes were set in rims of dark flesh, and the hand shook as it came away.

"It's Mr. Smith!" gasped Miss Jennifer.

"It's Robert Aldershot," Miss Rachel corrected. "And he certainly looks ghastly. I wonder if he ever saw the bandy-legged man."

Robert Aldershot was answering Monica; they could see his lips move, and the hand made a weak gesture when he finished speaking. But the voice, if there weas a voice, didn't penetrate the pane.

Monica burst out: "I'm not, I tell you. I never was. He's low and brutal and mean. I wouldn't touch him with a ten-foot pole."

The man's colorless lips moved briefly.

Monica leaned toward him, putting a hand on the mahogany bedside table with its array of bottles. Her sulky mouth was tight. "Yes, I must have been crazy to have let him go to Uncle Reuben. I admit that I must have been out of my head. Forget that. It gave Mr. Tommy Hale some very peculiar ideas about his own importance, including a delusion that he's about to become wealthy."

The man's head jerked up abruptly; the shaking hand cut off the rest of what Monica would have said.

But Monica drew away as the man spoke. She said, almost inaudibly to the Misses Murdock: "I didn't ask any details. I didn't want to hear his silly bragging nonsense."

The man sat straight and used what was obviously a great deal of his little strength in talking to her. A few of his words came through; *something damnable . . . if I weren't so helpless . . . where Florence made her mistake . . . little old lady . . . valuable . . .*

Miss Jennifer clutched Miss Rachel's hand. "Do you think he knows, somehow, that we followed Florence MacConnell?"

Miss Rachel shook her head absently, intent upon what Monica was saying: "I'll see what I can do." The sulky green eyes drifted from the man's face and rested on the window, and Miss Rachel felt her heart pound. If Monica saw them . . .

"Come away," Miss Jennifer whispered.

"I tried to make friends with her," Monica said. "I'll see where it leads."

"She's fooled you, Rachel," Miss Jennifer panted as they hurried away on the grass the fringed the drive. "Oh do be careful! Did you hear her? That friendliness you were so pleased with was all a fraud. Either Florence MacConnell recognized us and pretended she hadn't, or else he knew you when you were there today. And if you go away alone with that white haired hussy—"

"She didn't mention *me*," Miss Rachel panted back.

"Don't defend her!"

The night swallowed them, and there was only the sound of the cat, who was infected with the unusualness of the adventure. It was a long, long walk, but at least the return trip was downhill, and the road was paved to perfection.

It was almost three when they crept wearily into Mrs. Simpson's yard and went cautiously up the walk to the front porch. The wind was getting an early-morning freshness to it, and the stars seemed faded, ever so little, in the blackness overhead. The last of Mrs. Simpson's petunias breathed fragrance at them as they passed. Miss Jennifer was moaning with a blistered heel.

They had no key with them, since Mrs. Simpson had said casually that she never locked up; it wasn't necessary here.

The door opened into the pitch-blackness of the hall, and they felt their way to the staircase. The cat scampered ahead. Miss Rachel wondered who it was had let Samantha out twice. Mrs. Simpson's front door, which wasn't locked because it wasn't necessary, was being overworked by her prowling guests. Mrs. Simpson, innocent lady, would be the last to suspect.

They undressed in the dark and got into bed. Miss Jennifer whimpered at the cold sheets, her hot blistered heel, and the aching tiredness which she declared infected every bone of her body.

"I can't stand any more of this, Rachel. Positively. Don't ask it of me." She pulled the covers over her ears and sighed.

Miss Rachel stared at the dark and thought deeply. She had scarcely heard Jennifer's complaint. And she didn't know then, of course, just how much more terror and tiredness poor Jennifer was to endure.

Chapter VII

Miss Rachel peered at her sister with one sleepy eye. Miss Jennifer made a religion of getting up early, so it was natural that she had been downstairs and about while Rachel slept.

"Mrs. Simpson's what?"

"Crying in the kitchen," Miss Jennifer repeated. "Do get up, Rachel. This house has an uneasy atmosphere. Miss MacConnell keeps peeping out of her door every time I go past. Mrs. Simpson is making soup for lunch and crying over it."

"Onions," Miss Rachel suggested because she was sleepy.

"Not onions," Miss Jennifer said. "Onions make your eyes water. They don't make you sob and gulp air in as though the world was coming to an end."

"Did you ask about it?"

Miss Jennifer made her mouth prim. "Of course not. She's trying to control herself. The worst I could do would be to come out baldly and ask what the matter was."

Miss Rachel slid out of bed and stood up in a voluminous nightgown of baby pink flannel. Her white hair framed a face as rosy as a child's. She yawned daintily, then went searching for fresh petticoats. A half-hour later, neatly dressed in a morning gown of dimity, white hair neat and eyes curious, she tapped at the kitchen door.

Mrs. Simpson turned red eyes to her and gave a halfhearted, watery smile. "Good morning. Would you like breakfast now? An omelet, maybe?"

"A bit of toast and some fruit," Miss Rachel said, seeing the kitchen taken up with luncheon preparations. "I'm sorry to have been late. I don't deserve any breakfast."

"Nonsense. I'd have slept in myself if I could." She sniffled and put the coffee on to heat. "Such a night! I doubt if I had my eyes shut for an hour of it."

Mrs. Simpson shook her head dolefully, as though the subject were too grievous to carry further. "A bit of fruit, did you say? Here's a jar of apricots fresh opened—put them up myself this summer. Now—there's the doorbell! Wouldn't it be? Will you mind the toast for a minute?"

Miss Rachel was still minding the toast when Mrs. Simpson came back hurriedly. "It's for you, Miss Murdock. Monica Aldershot wants to see you."

Miss Rachel felt a trifle shy about meeting Monica. She wondered guiltily for a moment whether she and Jennifer had left footprints or anything. Then she was looking into Monica's green eyes, crinkling with friendliness.

"You little minx!" Miss Rachel thought hotly, remembering Monica's promise to her brother to cultivate somebody—obviously Miss Rachel, since here she was, cultivating.

"Good morning!" Monica cried. "Do you feel like trying San Cayetano with me? It's glorious outside—sun and windy smells." She put out a hand. "Come along. You'll love it."

In the rather poor light of the hall Monica's platinum hair

was like a halo, the color of her lipstick frosty and alive. She was an excellent actress. Miss Rachel thought to herself that no one would know she was motivated by duplicity. The green eyes shone with candor. "Of course you can come," she coaxed. "Get your things on."

"It will take me a minute," Miss Rachel said, going upstairs. She put in more than a minute quieting Jennifer, who prophesied mayhem and worse. Then she came down again, neatly wrapped and bonneted, to find Monica looking with very thoughtful eyes at the cat.

Samantha was on the lowest step, licking her paws.

"You do get around, don't you?" Monica said softly and glanced up. Just for an instant the friendliness was gone, and Miss Rachel knew unmistakably that they were playing a game, a deadly game—and much more deadly for her because she was so completely in the dark. "Ready so soon?" Monica turned and led the way outside.

They got into a low blue coupé. Monica drove expertly. They hadn't gone far when she said absently: "I was admiring your cat."

Miss Rachel smiled agreeably. There didn't seem to be much else to do.

"He's quite distinctive."

"Naughty, though," Miss Rachel said placidly. "Runs away at night."

Monica shot her an odd glance, and some of the suspicion seemed to leave her. "Tomcats do, of course. The nature of the brutes."

Miss Rachel kept still and looked at the scenery.

To her surprise they turned on an unfamiliar road some distance short of the Aldershot driveway.

"I'm going to stop at the tenant house for a minute," Monica explained. "I'm looking for my uncle, and he may be there."

"He's the gentleman in the wheel chair?"

"Yes. Like your cat, though, he gets about. There's a graveled pathway through the grove from our house here. He has a—a sort of shed for some of his things near by."

They had come within sight of a small pleasant bungalow painted white, with shutters stained green. The porch railing held a row of potted plants, somewhat overgrown. There was a look of emptiness behind windows, of neglect in the grassy yard and the porch with its surf of dust. Miss Rachel recalled in that instant the things she had heard: that Florence MacConnell had lived here with her father, had been forced to move when her father was discharged by the Aldershots, and that now the property was vacant.

Monica pulled the car to a halt and tootled impatiently on the horn. There was no sign of life. She opened the door on the far side and got out and stood looking at the house and frowning. "I suppose he's out hunting spi——" She didn't complete the word. Her uncle had come into sight in the wheel chair.

He nodded to Miss Rachel and turned to his niece. "Well, Monica, this is a surprise. A little early for you, isn't it?"

"I want you to tell Krug to let Tommy go."

"Let Tommy—— My dear, you don't let farm workers go these days. You coddle and humor and overpay them to keep them from running off into war industries. A raise in Tommy's wages might be managed. But as to firing him, I wouldn't advise it."

Someone else had come round the corner of the bungalow, someone quite new to Miss Rachel, though there was a look of familiarity to him. He had the green, direct gaze of Monica and

Uncle Reuben. He was about eighteen, perhaps a trifle younger. He had a jar in his hands in which a dark mass scampered and wriggled.

Reuben Carder looked over his shoulder at him. "Harley's helping me this morning. He can reach the more inaccessible places."

Harley grinned. "I'm really studying Uncle Reuben. If I'm going to write I've got to know all sorts."

"Miss Murdock, this is my brother Harley." Monica looked at her uncle. "You *are* going to fire Tommy. I'm telling you to."

"You didn't want him fired yesterday," Reuben said gently.

"I'll bet they had another fight," Harley put in. "It's cheap, Sis, getting back at him that way."

"Shut up." Monica studied her uncle coldly. "I have a voice, do I not, in what goes on here?"

"Of course, Monica. It's your land—yours and your brothers', and while Robert is ill and Harley under age you should rightly have the major vote in anything. I'm merely advising you." Reuben's brown face with its chalk-white mustache was full of mild rebuke. "I'm your hired man as much as Tommy is. If you insist that he be let go, I'll have Krug do it."

Something in Monica's manner wilted suddenly. There was silence, while Reuben waited and Harley watched the scampering mass in the jar with amused eyes.

"I'll see you later about this," Monica said finally.

Reuben Carder watched his niece with a humorous expression which Miss Rachel didn't like. The girl's indecision seemed to amuse him. There was a cold streak in his nature, obviously, which found fun in other people's discomfiture.

Monica looked at Miss Rachel, still sitting in the car. "We'll go for our drive now. We've delayed long enough."

Miss Rachel looked cautiously over her shoulder as they sped out of the yard. Carder was watching them. Monica's young brother had turned back toward the house, walking with an easy slouch, the jar with its dark contents hanging in one hand.

"Is your uncle an entomologist?" Miss Rachel asked.

Monica shook her head. "There isn't anything scientific in what he's doing. He raises birds and fowl, you know. You saw his pigeons. One day he noticed how they relished spiders when they caught them. He trapped a few spiders and fed them to the birds. He's just—just gotten into it gradually. He has a spider hut in the grove and has, I guess, thousands of the things there." She drove in silence for a little while. "I've never been inside it, though Harley says that it's interesting."

The idea of a man who collected spiders to feed to his pigeons made Miss Rachel's skin creep a little.

"Has he ever been bitten?"

"I don't know. I don't think so. He's pretty careful. Some of the things are poisonous—tarantulas and black widows. He doesn't feed those to the birds, of course."

"It's a strange hobby."

"My uncle is a little strange," Monica answered impersonally. "He's handicapped because of his illness. He can't do the things most normal people do. He's bitter, subconsciously and without realizing it."

They had passed the Aldershot home at a distance. The road climbed here in a long sweep, and the gash it made up the side of San Cayetano was straightening out ahead. San Cayetano seemed to be rushing at them like some great beast moving among the orange trees. Long blue meadows and highlands, topped with crags, hung over them, and there was a smell of sage and dry grasses and hot sun. A heady dizziness came over

Miss Rachel. It was, as Monica promised it would be, a little like flying.

The road climbed and swung, and they came into the clear and looked down. The valley was like a receding floor under them. Far on its other side the tiny oil wells were toys set out along the little hills; their silvered tanks were thimbles in the sunlight; their spires were of thread. The village was made for dolls; the roads were pencil lines upon which little bugs crept.

Sun and winy air were everywhere, and the orange trees made a green carpet she might have put her foot upon.

In the midst of this intoxication of beauty the car rounded a curve and shuddered to a halt under Monica's quick grip on the brake.

Miss Rachel, somewhat shaken, looked ahead. Some three feet beyond the radiator of the car a grille of new boards made a barrier. Monica turned to her slowly. On Monica's chin was a red bruise where she had struck the steering wheel, and her pompadour of curls had fallen awry.

"I'll be damned," she said.

"Is it the end of your road?" Miss Rachel asked.

The girl seemed to come out of some abstraction. "Our road? We've never found the end of our road." She laughed. "Someone's put this here. It's a mistake, of course. I'm going to tear it down."

Monica got out and took car tools from the rumble compartment. She attacked the barrier with a tire iron and a wrench. The stout boards shook under her blows, and Miss Rachel could see the sweat on Monica's face and the bitter strain about her mouth. When she paused to rest she was shaking. But the barrier stood.

Miss Rachel got out of the car. There was more here than a

girl's impatience at having her drive spoiled. There were desperation, purpose, a hint of anger. Monica brushed back her hair as Miss Rachel approached, and she grinned shakily.

"Be through in a minute."

"You aren't making much progress. I'm afraid it's past your strength."

Monica looked at the boards, at the stout timbers to which they were nailed. She kicked at the supports with her suède oxford. "Like a rock." She drew a deep breath. "Now it's all spoiled. You won't be able to see San Cayetano after all."

"I've seen a great deal." Miss Rachel looked out into sunny immensity. "Your valley is beautiful when one gets up here and looks down at it. It's—it's as though someone had arranged it from a distance to be quite perfect, as though it had been drawn to scale and then transplanted." She paused. "It's hard to explain what I mean."

"I know what you mean. I've felt that way. To get away and see it without any detail—any people in it—makes it seem a little world for gods." Her tone held something of bitterness, of passion.

In the silence that followed, the faint chug-chug of a heavy motor drifted up to them. Far below, at the edge of the orange grove, a tractor came into view, circled, and went back among the trees. Monica turned her face away, as though there were something in it that Miss Rachel must not see.

But Miss Rachel pressed the point. "Is that machine working on your land?"

"Part of it. The west grove. We—we have more than one tractor. More than one hired man too," she added, as if to herself: some hurtful, secret reminder.

"I suppose your people have been with you for a long time."

"Some of them."

"Are there—are there very many older men able to work in the groves?"

Monica's eyes slid sidewise; Miss Rachel felt their regard. "Older men are about all we have left. A few younger men have been deferred from Army service because of dependents, but most of them will go eventually."

Miss Rachel could think of no way to bring Jeff Woodley into the conversation. And yet somehow, through Monica, she had hoped to meet him.

Monica had turned back toward the car. "I wish I might have shown you the things I'd planned to. There is a slate pit farther up. It's a natural formation, though it's been deepened by mining. The Indians used it in its original state as a place to put their enemies. The slate is smooth, you see. Once in it you couldn't get out."

"How dreadful," Miss Rachel said. "Has anyone been in it—anyone since those early days, that is?"

Monica's glance clouded. "A man named Hale, the father of one of our workers, fell into it. That was twenty years ago, though. The peculiar part of it was that Hale had owned the mountain lands and had just recently sold them to my father. He hunted often up here. He should have known his danger."

"Do you mean that the fall killed him?"

"They weren't sure." Monica was looking at the ground, where the toe of her shoe had made a scuffling mark. Miss Rachel felt that Hale's death was something that Monica had thought about before, that something in it repelled while it intrigued her. "Someone told me once that he'd shot himself in a hunting accident and was dragging himself home—that that was why he fell into the pit. I don't know. I was a baby then."

What an ugly story it was, Miss Rachel thought, and full of so many possibilities for lingering hatred and violence.

"Perhaps if you'd see the pit——" Monica said and stopped.

If I could see the pit . . . The altitude, Miss Rachel thought, had made her giddy. She could fairly see the pit, the smooth slate pit opening just in front of her, and she imagined it as a hole without any bottom whatever.

CHAPTER VIII

MONICA HAD difficulty in turning the car; at one point Miss Rachel looked off into blue space and held her breath, waiting for the wheels to topple. Eventually, though, they were swung round and headed downward.

"I want to see Krug about this business," Monica said. "Do you mind stopping at the house for a minute on the way back? Krug is apt to be off somewhere in the groves if I wait too long."

"I don't mind at all." Miss Rachel's mind busied itself with possibilities of prowling.

They turned at the Aldershot drive, cleared the veiling of eucalyptus and pepper trees and came in sight of the lawn. At what she saw there Miss Rachel sat up quite straight and swallowed. She grew a little pale.

"Now who can that be?" Monica wondered.

It was Lieutenant Mayhew, large and brown and stonily official. Facing him in a semicircle were Reuben Carder, Harley Aldershot—who still carried the jar of prisoned spiders—and a third man in overalls whom Miss Rachel didn't know. Mayhew's car was parked at the edge of the gravel, and Edson, his favorite assistant, was putting letters and papers into a suitcase. There was a studied ruthlessness to Mayhew's air, and when he looked up and saw Monica and Miss Rachel there was no friendliness came over him.

"He's going to be very difficult," Miss Rachel thought. "He's seen Jennifer in the village, because obviously he expected to meet me."

She felt the impalement of Mayhew's stare at their passing; she knew that a guilty blush was making her cheeks scarlet.

"Whoever he is, he can wait," Monica said, skirting Mayhew's car. "I'm going to find Krug."

They rounded the house, followed the graveled drive between pens of ducks and peafowl, and came into a cleared paved space before a long garage. The memory of the way Mayhew had looked at them still froze Miss Rachel's marrow, but this, she saw, was an opportunity not likely to come again.

"While you're away I'll walk about a bit," she said, giving it a touch of asking permission.

"Of course." Monica waved hastily to the pens of fowl. "Look at Uncle Reuben's collection. He has hundreds of birds; some species you haven't seen before, most likely."

She went off in the direction of a group of outbuildings, and Miss Rachel slipped from the car and made a brief show of staring in at the strutting birds. Then she went quickly to the garage. The doors of several empty cubicles were open; she stepped through one and looked about. The building had little in the way of inside partitions; spaces for six cars were set apart by timber framing. Two coupés were at her right, one black and one dull green; to the left, at the end and shadowed by a closed door, stood a long sedan.

Miss Rachel felt her breath stop. Her mind had gone back to the hill on Sutter Street, to the swoop of a big car, the flying body of a man. Here sat the car in the dark—quiet, cold. It was as though she had come face to face with the murderer himself.

She felt her own limbs tremble as she walked along the side of the car to its front fenders. Here it was—if this were the car as she believed it to be—there should be some evidence of the impact. She had just bent toward the dusty surface when voices outside warned her to be quiet.

She slid down out of sight, a crumpled heap of taffeta and starched petticoats. The head lamp of the car faced her like a big eye, and in it she could see her own white hair and blue bonnet and skin like paper. She felt a shiver of nervousness. The voices were coming in.

"—couldn't help him any. If I'd knowed what was comin' I'd of stopped it." The voice was illiterate, dull, heavy with hopelessness. For some reason Miss Rachel thought of the overalled man she had seen in the group on the lawn. "'Tain't any good, him askin' me over and over. What you don't know, you don't know, that's all."

"It's funny Tim didn't tell you anything."

"Sure it was funny. Tim made out like he wanted a vacation in town. I didn't know he had an idea of tryin' to find Mr. Aldershot. He asked me to find out where Florence MacConnell'd gone. I said I reckoned the MacConnells would go back to Salinas, where they come from. He looked at me kind of queer. We were settin' at dinner. 'What makes you think Florence is with her dad?' he asked me. But he wouldn't say any more."

"When are you going down to Los Angeles?" This second voice was Tommy's. It was not now cruel and ironic as when he had talked to Monica; it had a spent quality, as though the words went on while the mind was elsewhere.

"Soon's I get ready. These here detectives are takin' me down.

Takin' Tim's stuff, too, all his papers and letters and such. I guess they figger Tim wrote down what he meant to do. Whatever Tim had on his mind he kept there. I oughta know. Lived with him fifty years." There was a dry sob, hastily stifled. Miss Rachel stole a look from under the fender's wing. The overalled man's legs—he must be Jeff Woodley—were just inside the shadow of the door; Tommy's huskier pair kicked aimlessly at the frame.

"What had Tim been doing lately?" Tommy asked after a space of silence.

"Nothin'."

"I don't mean work. I mean was there anything a little unusual about the way he passed his time?"

"He got so he liked to hike a little, takin' it easy on his leg, o' course. Said it kept him from gettin' stiff."

"Did he ever act afraid, nervous, jumpy?"

"Nope. He just never was afraid of a thing from the time we was kids. If he got an idea in his head, though, he'd hang onto it like a bulldog. Couldn't never change him. Couldn't scare him, either."

Into Miss Rachel's mind came the picture of the bandy-legged man, patient in his long vigil under the rosebushes.

Tommy asked the question she herself had just thought of: "What did he think of Florence MacConnell?"

"I don't know. Tim knew somethin' about that girl he wouldn't never tell me. It happened when he was first hurt and was laid up till his leg healed. He used to lay out in the sun up at our shack—as much sun as you get in the lee of this here mountain—and he was so still-like; I guess he heard somethin'. I don't know. He used to say she didn't have the morals of a she-cat."

There was curious, stifled silence on Tommy's part. Then he said jerkily: "Had he—had he ever seen her with anybody?"

"Can't say. Guess he heard or saw somethin'. I guess he caught on when she first began to make up to Mr. Aldershot. I never give it any notice till he told me."

"Do you think he knew they had gone away together at first?"

"No, I don't. He inquired a lot; I know he pumped Johnny at the grocery store and old man Squeers at the service station. He wrote one letter to Florence's dad in Salinas. You know, I've got a hunch it was old man MacConnell told him where Florence was. And he watched and seen that Mr. Aldershot was with her."

"Did you find out what Mr. Aldershot has to say about it?"

"Yep. Same as me. Didn't know a thing; ain't seen Tim since he left here more'n two months ago."

"Why did Aldershot come home just at this time? Did he make any explanation of that?"

"I don't know. All that Mr. Mayhew told me was that he claims he hadn't seen my brother." Old Jeff's voice broke on the last word, and he began frankly to cry.

Miss Rachel, hearing the deep heartbroken sobs, felt the burden of bitter self-condemnation. If she had called the police at the first sight of the bandy-legged man's peculiar actions, had had him taken away and forced to explain himself, he would have been alive now. She remembered her indecision in the matter, her own ineffectual watching, her lack of quickness in making sure of the identity of the car.

Tommy said awkwardly: "Well, you'd better be packing. Come on and I'll help." The steps of the two men went away together, and their sound must have covered the quiet approach of another.

Miss Rachel rose and smoothed her taffeta skirt and adjusted her bonnet by looking into the silvered head lamp.

She found herself looking at another face beside her own, a brown square face with a quiet anger in it.

"H-h-hello, Lieutenant," she managed.

"Don't lieutenant me," Mayhew said. His bitter glance went over the car. "I suppose you've dusted this for fingerprints."

"You know I can't do that."

"There are a great many things which the general public is supposed to leave for the police. Including murders. We're supposed to work for our money, you know."

She looked very meek. "I know."

"You may have made a great deal of trouble for us, coming up here and frightening the suspects."

Her eyes brightened. "Then they *are* suspects?"

"Who do you think would have gone to the trouble of killing Tim Woodley to keep him from seeing Robert Aldershot? Obviously someone who knew what Woodley was up to. It all leads here." He slapped the fender heavily with a glove. "Come on in, Edson, and get busy on this thing. Now." He had turned back to Miss Rachel. "What did this young Hale have to say to old Jeff?"

Miss Rachel read hopeful signs of relenting in Mayhew's face. She related the conversation between Tommy and Jeff and tried to make it sound valuable.

Edson had rolled back the garage door, and in the increased light Mayhew looked impassive and thoughtful.

"What about this car?" he asked. "Do you think it's the one you saw on Sutter Street?"

"It's the same type. I—I suppose you'll be able to find out for sure with the equipment you have."

"Yes, we have our uses," Mayhew said, but not ungraciously. "If Woodley was struck by it and carried away in it there will have to be traces of some sort. Meanwhile, I suggest you go back to the village and I'll see you there later. We may be able to keep quiet the fact that we know each other, at least for a time."

"That might prove valuable."

He watched as Edson opened a suitcase containing a packed array of scientific equipment. "Begin with fingerprints," he said. Quietly he added: "Here comes your Miss Aldershot. You'd better leave me."

Monica met Miss Rachel by the car. There had been an abrupt change in her. Under the wind-tossed pompadour of curls her face was waxy. Her breath was shallow and labored. She stared at Miss Rachel as though she had forgotten bringing her here, then opened the door mechanically.

"Get in, please."

It was strange, driving back to Mrs. Simpson's in the noonday warmth with Monica a white automaton beside her. They had entered the village before Monica spoke. "Did you hear any of that?"

Miss Rachel skirted the equivocal question. "Any of what, my dear?"

"That—that awfulness about the man who used to work for us. His name was Woodley, and he's been murdered in Los Angeles." She bit her lips, stared hard against the sun.

"I believe I did hear something of the sort." Miss Rachel wondered whether there was any use in carrying on a pretense with Monica. Had Monica's brother really seen and recognized Miss Rachel, as his conversation the previous night would indicate? "It's been a shock to you, hasn't it?"

Monica looked round to face her and seemed about to speak. Some deep emotion fled through her eyes like a shadow on a stream. "She's beautiful," Miss Rachel thought in the instant of waiting, "beautiful and proud. Proud enough, perhaps, to be quite ruthless." She felt a little sorry for Tommy.

Monica turned without having spoken. The car slid to a stop before Mrs. Simpson's gate. Mrs. Simpson looked out briefly at the sound of their stopping; her face was frankly tearful now.

"What's wrong with her?" Monica asked. "Could she—but of course she couldn't have heard about Tim yet. And, besides, I think she scarcely knew him."

Miss Rachel stepped from the car. "Thanks for taking me up the mountain. Even though we didn't get to the top, it was lovely."

Monica, deep in her own perplexity, seemed not to hear. She was still looking at the door behind which Mrs. Simpson's red eyes had disappeared.

Miss Rachel waited an instant, and then, taking the girl's silence for a tacit good-by, she turned toward the path.

The car door slammed, and then Monica was hurrying beside her. For a moment Miss Rachel thought that Monica must have some idea of accompanying her to the door, perhaps to speak to Mrs. Simpson. Then, raising her eyes, she saw the face that looked down at them from an upper window.

It was Florence MacConnell. Her dark hair was swept up and back and topped with a modish little hat. She was pulling on her gloves. And her eyes, fixed on Monica, were calculating and defiant.

Monica rang Mrs. Simpson's bell, and then without waiting to be admitted she flung open the door and ran for the stairs. At the same time there came to Miss Rachel's ears some sort of hurrying movement from the second floor.

Mrs. Simpson was in the archway to the living room, and

Miss Rachel saw that she held a sheet of letter paper in one hand and that it was spotted with tears. "What is it?" she asked Monica. "Is something wrong?"

Monica was already at the landing. She glanced back briefly. "I'm sorry, Mrs. Simpson. I have to see this person." Then she was out of sight; her steps sounded in the upper hall.

They waited, Mrs. Simpson dabbing her eyes and Miss Rachel listening for what might ensue when the two young women met. The moments dragged out to a lengthy silence, and then Monica reappeared, coming down slowly.

"How could she get away so quickly?" she demanded of Mrs. Simpson. "I saw her from out of doors. But she isn't in any of the rooms up there."

Mrs. Simpson compressed her mouth. "Don't you think that you folks might leave the girl alone, Miss Aldershot? Even though her father made some mistake in his work, or even if he criticized your uncle for keeping that little houseful of bugs, as folks say he does, must you be persecuting——?"

Monica cut her off. "I'm not persecuting her, Mrs. Simpson. I'm just trying to find out if she's—if she's as foul as my brother thinks she is!"

CHAPTER IX

Mrs. Simpson swallowed, and her eyes widened with shock. "Florence? She's always seemed such a nice girl."

"I know." Monica's frosty-red mouth seemed suddenly tired. "I shouldn't have said that. Perhaps Florence has reasons for the way she's acted. I wish, though"—she glanced behind her at the upper-floor landing—"I wish she'd tell them to Robert."

"I don't understand about your brother," Mrs. Simpson said primly. "Do you mean that he and Florence are engaged or something?"

"They're married." She said it flatly, without emphasis. "They've been married for more than two months. He didn't tell us. We thought he intended to go to an Eastern sanitarium for treatment for his heart condition. He—they only went as far as Los Angeles." She put up a hand and pressed her temple, as though she were confused and weary. "It seems as though Tim Woodley went there to try to get in touch with Robert. No one knows why. Tim was killed, struck by a car, and—and then taken away and murdered. Horribly."

Miss Rachel perceived what the less agile mind of Mrs. Simpson hadn't taken in—that Monica was on a thin edge of disaster. She hurried to the girl and took her hand.

"Come and sit down, my dear. Mrs. Simpson, have you a bit of brandy in the house?"

Monica looked at her whitely. "Thank you. Thank you so much."

Mrs. Simpson whimpered: "Now this, on top of all my other troubles!" and hurried away after the brandy.

Monica let herself be led to a chair and sank down upon it. Miss Rachel bent over her. "If you had seen Miss MacConnell what would you have said to her?"

"I'd have asked her why she married Robert secretly and took him away. If she did it knowingly, if it was part of this thing Robert suspects was planned far in advance, she's—she's more rotten than I had dreamed."

"And what does Robert think was planned?" Miss Rachel pressed.

"We don't know."

Was Monica lying? Miss Rachel scanned her closely for any sign of caution or evasion. Could Robert Aldershot suspect a plot and yet be entirely ignorant of its nature?

"I don't understand," Miss Rachel said.

"It's something we feel is there but can't bring out into the open." Monica took the brandy Mrs. Simpson offered and sipped it slowly. Then she sat quiet.

"I think Miss MacConnell left by the back stairs," Mrs. Simpson offered, and then without any visible cause burst into tears. Miss Rachel was about to suggest that she have a sip of her own brandy, when she continued: "Excuse me breaking down like this. It's my sister in Delaware. Just the two of us now, and she's taken bad with pneumonia. They've got her in an oxygen tent in the hospital and they don't think she'll live. I had a telegram asking me to come."

"I'm so sorry," Miss Rachel said, feeling the inadequacy of the words.

"That's why Miss MacConnell was leaving. I've hated to say anything to you ladies, since your sister came here for her own health and all." Mrs. Simpson dabbed her eyes fiercely and then did as Miss Rachel had hoped she would: took a drink of brandy. "But there's no use holding back any longer. I even thought of writing to say I couldn't come." She waved the tear-spotted sheet of letter paper. "It's no use. Joe wouldn't ever forgive me if Grace died and I hadn't even tried to see her."

"Of course you must go." Miss Rachel's thoughts faced the inevitable: the one place in San Cayetano where they could stay was being closed to her and Jennifer. "And don't worry about us. We'll make some sort of arrangements elsewhere while you're away."

"Oh, would you?" A smile lightened Mrs. Simpson's teary grief. "And it wouldn't be too much hardship for you?"

"Not at all."

"I don't know where you could stay hereabouts, but you might try the other towns down the valley. Santa Paula, for instance. Or Fillmore." She drew a deep breath and frowned a little. "Course they're not as dry as here."

"We'll make out somehow."

Finally reassured, Mrs. Simpson went off upstairs to pack. Monica also rose and after thanking Miss Rachel for her thoughtfulness walked toward the front door.

"Miss—Miss Aldershot."

Monica looked back at her.

"You heard Mrs. Simpson's plan to go East?"

"Yes. I'm sorry about her sister. Stupid of me to have been so wrapped up in my own affairs that I didn't tell her so."

"Would you rent us your tenant house?"

Monica's face seemed to congeal in its expression of incredulous surprise.

"My sister Jennifer needs the dry air and the altitude so badly," Miss Rachel said quickly. "I'm hoping we may be able to stay for a little while, at least. I thought—your tenant house is empty, isn't it?"

"Yes." Monica's eyes studied her curiously. "It isn't very well furnished, though, and I don't know how clean it is. Florence and her father moved out more than two months ago. It hasn't been opened since."

"We wouldn't mind that."

"There's something else. You saw my uncle there and you know of his peculiar hobby. He has a little house—more of a shed, really—where he keeps his collection, and it isn't far. You might be nervous, if you're afraid of spiders."

"I don't believe we'd be afraid, so long as he keeps them penned up."

"Harley says he's fixed them a glassed-in arrangement with a skylight. Much the effect of an aquarium, I gathered." She shivered slightly. "I think I'd better ask Robert's advice on renting the tenant house. If you don't mind waiting, I could let you know this afternoon."

"Very well."

As Monica went out Miss Jennifer came in. Miss Rachel tried to think of a way to tell her that they might move into the vicinity of Reuben Carder's spider hut and then decided to keep a diplomatic silence. Miss Jennifer had her stubborn streaks. It was just possible she would refuse to move.

They went upstairs together, and Miss Jennifer told Miss Rachel about the lieutenant. Mayhew had arrived shortly after Miss Rachel had gone away with Monica. There was more than a hint that Jennifer had made her the scapegoat for the whole affair, Miss Rachel reflected. She listened to Miss Jennifer's recital, filling in the gaps from what she knew of Jennifer's methods. At the end came a surprising bit of news. On her walk, from which she had just returned, Miss Jennifer had met Florence MacConnell going toward the bus depot.

"She was positively smirking," Miss Jennifer said. "She looked like a cat that had just finished off a whole cageful of canaries and was about to have whipped cream for dessert."

"She had slipped away from Monica Aldershot," Miss Rachel said. "I suppose that made her feel pretty triumphant."

"And she was singing," Miss Jennifer added. "Just as I came close to her she stopped smirking long enough to sing a little song under her breath. Really, she just glowed with a sort of spiteful success."

"Singing? What did she sing, Jennifer?"

"It was about love." Miss Jennifer hummed an experimental bar. "That's it. 'I Can't Give You Anything but Love, Baby.'"

"How very odd."

"I thought of asking if she had told the lieutenant she was leaving the village, and then I didn't. She was worried this morning; she kept peering out of her room at everyone that passed. That phone call must have changed things for her."

Miss Rachel put on a look of impatience. "What phone call, Jennifer?"

"I don't know *what* phone call. *A* phone call. The phone rang, and she flew downstairs and answered it before Mrs. Simpson could get out of the kitchen."

"And what did Miss MacConnell say?"

Jennifer looked very prim. "I didn't eavesdrop, Rachel."

"You'll have to, if you're going to be any good at this sort of thing," Miss Rachel said shamelessly. "That telephone call could have been very important. In fact, it *was* important. It cheered Florence MacConnell up and sent her hurrying out of town. You lost a valuable opportunity in not listening to her part of it."

"Well——"

"I thought so."

Miss Jennifer blushed. "Am I very hypocritical, Rachel?"

"That's beside the point, at least at present. What did she say?"

"I happened to hear two sentences. She said, 'You'll have to see my side of it too.' And later she said, 'I'm a poor girl.'"

Miss Rachel took time to think. "I believe that Miss MacConnell is a very mercenary young lady. If she's blackmailing someone, if she is so incredibly foolish as to try to get money out of a murderer——"

Miss Jennifer shivered. "Shouldn't we tell Lieutenant Mayhew about this, Rachel?"

"We shall tell him. He should be here very shortly."

Her prediction took form in about fifteen minutes with the arrival of Mayhew. Edson and the dead man's brother waited in his car; Miss Rachel looked down at them from the east window as Mayhew's bulky bigness vanished beneath the porch roof.

Mrs. Simpson being safely engaged in packing and her house helper checking the locks of windows on the upper floor, Miss Rachel took Mayhew into the parlor. Miss Jennifer joined them, having the important bit about the telephone call to relate. The cat came, too, smelled Mayhew's familiar legs, and sat looking at him and purring.

Mayhew scolded them at first. They took it meekly. Miss Jennifer was beginning to see Rachel's point about the lieutenant. He *did* seem to think that he had a corner on crime. "Wait," she thought, "until I tell him about Miss MacConnell. He'll be glad he's got us then."

Mayhew was surprisingly unglad. "Why didn't you follow her?" he asked.

"She was going in the direction of the bus depot and she was carrying a suitcase."

Mayhew walked out to the hall telephone and rang the depot. Turning back, he looked grim and joyless. "There isn't a bus from here today until three o'clock this afternoon. Miss Mac-Connell—or anyone like her—hasn't been near the depot, hasn't bought a ticket, isn't waiting for the bus."

"Oh," said Miss Jennifer, reflecting on the perfidious conduct of the girl.

Mayhew lost no time in ringing the local sheriff's office and asking that a watch be kept for Miss MacConnell. Coming back to the parlor, he let Miss Jennifer tell him about the telephone call and the song Florence had been singing. He wrote most of it down in a brown notebook.

"Now," he said, shutting the book and putting it away, "about the car in the Aldershot garage. We're pretty sure it's the one we're after. We scraped some bloodstains from under the rug in the rear seat. The rug's new, by the way—we're trying to trace that too. We'll have the blood analyzed and then we'll know for sure. There were some woolen shreds caught in a tear in the front fender. They'll have to be compared scientifically, of course, but they appear to match the clothing of Mr. Woodley."

"You haven't explained what led you here," Miss Rachel said hesitatingly.

"The man himself," Mayhew answered, passing up an opportunity to remind Miss Rachel that she should have done this. "He had once served as a deputy sheriff here in San Cayetano, and his prints were on file in the substation in Los Angeles. That was sheer luck, of course. Otherwise we'd still be stumbling around in the dark."

"Speaking of fingerprints," Miss Rachel hurried to say guiltily, "I was wondering if there might have been some in the car."

"There are. Thousands of them. It seems the sedan is a general car that's used by whoever takes a notion he needs it."

"And where was the car supposed to have been during the time it must have been used to run down Mr. Woodley?"

"In the garage, though it wasn't, obviously. No one at the Aldershot place seems to remember seeing it that day. This is easily explained. There was heavy, low fog during that morning, and a continuing driveway back of the garages, through the groves, is practically invisible unless you're directly on it."

"Have you fixed any definite limits on the time it must have been gone?"

"It's a large, fast car. Figuring the run into Los Angeles at about an hour and a quarter, another hour for what was done to Woodley, a second run back here, you'd have a total of about four hours to be accounted for. That's not a minimum figure. Woodley was buried, or rather dirt was scattered over him, in a spot which is just off the direct route back here. It might have been a little less than four hours—though we can't know, of course, just how long the murderer waited until Woodley put himself into a position to be run down."

"What about the Aldershots and their employees? Any alibis?"

Mayhew laughed briefly and bitterly, drew the notebook from his pocket, and jerked its leaves apart. "Do you want to be amused? Here, read them. They literally aren't worth the sheet of paper they're written on."

She saw the neat entries in Mayhew's big masculine script:

Robert Aldershot: *Suffered a heart attack of unusual duration during the night at the house in Los Angeles. Wife insisted on their immediate return to San Cayetano just in case things were going to be serious. They arrived in wife's car in early-morning hours before daybreak. He still had a key, which the wife used to admit them to the house. They disturbed no one. He took a sleeping tablet, slept heavily until noon, when he was awakened by the housekeeper. He accounts for the fact that no one saw him in that his room was presumed empty, and no one would ordinarily look into it except a servant in cleaning.*

"What did Florence MacConnell have to say about their return from Los Angeles?" Miss Rachel asked.

"Her story was the same. It could easily be true. He's subject to severe but passing attacks of palpitation."

Miss Rachel continued with Mayhew's notes.

Monica Aldershot: *On this morning* [Miss Rachel added mentally: *of all mornings*] *Miss Aldershot decided to have a herb garden. She went away in rough clothes with a spade to a cleared spot in the grove and worked there the entire morning. No one saw her there, so far as she knows.*

Harley Aldershot: *Took a portable typewriter to an ex-tool shed some distance from house and tried to write. Returned to house twice during morning for a drink of water and some pie. Saw no one. Thought that he may have heard the car returning but isn't sure. Housekeeper unable to remember whether pie was missing.*

Reuben Carder: *Spent morning of murder in his hobby of collecting spiders. Claims to have additional spiders to prove it—but spiders don't talk. Apparently confined to wheel chair but can operate a car. Admitted this after prints were found in car. Couldn't remember whether he had been near garages the morning of the crime.*

Amos Krug: *Superintendent of Aldershot properties, handles pay rolls, employment; also acts as general purchasing agent. Claims to have been checking on some new nursery stock at the western end of the groves. He admitted taking a spade with him to examine root development. Saw no one until after noon.*

Thomas Hale: *laborer. Ran a tractor part of the morning in upper levels of grove near mountain lands. Amount of work done cannot be checked this late. Says he waved at a figure in distance below which he believes was Harley's. No check on this, due to fog.*

Jeff Woodley: *Making repairs on a tractor in shop behind the barn. Does not recall hearing or seeing anything suspicious. Housekeeper called him for cup of coffee at ten-thirty.*

Mrs. Letitia Jackson: *housekeeper. She and Jeff Woodley verify each other.*

CHAPTER X

"OF COURSE, as Mr. Carder pointed out," Mayhew continued with an ironic tilt to his mouth, "it is possible that an unknown, a stranger, could have sneaked in and taken the car without too much trouble. Someone, Mr. Carder thought, who'd had an old grudge against Woodley and had a sudden urge to wipe it out."

"Ridiculous!" cried Miss Jennifer. "Why, even I wouldn't swallow that! It would be a miraculous coincidence that an old grudge should catch up with Woodley just as he was about to see Robert Aldershot on a mysterious errand."

"Mr. Carder had an answer to that one too. He suggested that Tim Woodley had gone to Aldershot for protection against this stranger."

"Protection? To a man practically dead with heart trouble?"

"I pointed that out to him. He murmured something about mental and spiritual protection, but it was weak."

"Have you found any hint," Miss Rachel put in, "of what it might have been that took Woodley to Los Angeles?"

"Not so far. He seems, on the strength of his brother's story, to have been a long time about doing anything. He began trying to trace Aldershot more than a month ago. There's a rough map, incidentally, in his papers which shows an outline of the Aldershot properties. Some of the back-country boundaries, the mountain lands, are vague, sketched in with dots. Jeff Woodley doesn't ever remember seeing it in his brother's possession and thinks it must be something he acquired recently. There's nothing on the map, however, which isn't a common and easily recognizable feature of the landscape."

"Do you think it's one that Tim Woodley drew freehand, or is it a copy? Or can you tell?"

Mayhew frowned in reflection. "I think—somehow—that it's a copy. Some of the lettering on it doesn't match any of Woodley's writing. The paper is thin and the letters shake a trifle, as though they were traced."

"Could I see it?"

After an instant's hesitation, as though he were afraid she might be putting something over on him, Mayhew drew an envelope from an inner pocket of his coat. "This map seemed so promising I took it out of the rest of his stuff which we're taking to Los Angeles." From the envelope he extracted a thin and tattered piece of paper.

"Hmmmm. Well worn," Miss Rachel commented. "But why is part of it drawn in red and part in common pencil?"

"I asked Jeff Woodley about that. He says, so far as he can see, it's a division of the Aldershot lands according to the time they were bought by the family. The black lines enclose a section of valley land which was bought by old man Aldershot at about the turn of the century. The red lines mark a later acquisition."

Miss Rachel stared at the little map on which San Cayetano was outlined with feathery wiggles. She could see with a glance that the mountain had been drawn in accurately so far as the contour of its base facing the valley was concerned. Far to the right, near what should be the highest levels of its meadows, was a black dot like a small, malignant eye.

"That," Mayhew said, putting a big nail on the dot, "should represent a pit that's up there, according to Jeff Woodley."

"It's labeled. Rather faintly." Miss Rachel held the thin paper toward the light from the windows. Waveringly, in old-fashioned capital lettering, was written: *Sl. Pit.* She remembered suddenly the ugly story of Tommy Hale's father, who had fallen into the pit after a supposed hunting accident, on land of which he should have known every inch. Monica had only hinted at the story's possibilities for smoldering hatred.

"There's no road drawn on the mountain," Miss Rachel commented.

"Jeff Woodley noticed that. It seemed to puzzle him."

In the map's lower half the Aldershot home was indicated by a crooked rectangle, with the name *Aldershot* in rather illiterate script, and the long street that approached it drawn in with a single stroke of a pencil.

Miss Rachel spoke after a while of silent thought. "It looks to me as though part of the map was a copy and part was drawn by Woodley himself, added somewhat carelessly. The outline of the mountain, the lettering of its name and of the pit are exact— even meticulous. The part showing the Aldershot home and surrounding lands seems hurried and inaccurate. The house, for instance, is shown as being directly on the street. Outside of the mountain lands, there hasn't been any attempt to judge distances relatively. And the word *Aldershot* is scribbled in."

"That part of it matches other samples we have of Tim Woodley's writing. I agree that only part of the map seems to be copied. But copied from what?"

"You might find out when the mountain road was built," Miss Rachel said. "That may give us a lead as far as time is concerned."

"I understand that you and Miss Aldershot were on the road this morning."

"Not very far." She told him of the barrier and of Monica's peculiar reaction to it. "I got the feeling that it was an act, a game, in which I was supposed to play an unsuspecting part."

"Be sure whatever game it is is a deep one. And not for fun," Mayhew warned. "Don't expose yourself to danger. I suppose there's no use in suggesting that you go back to Los Angeles?" he added with small hope.

"*I'm* going to try to find Miss MacConnell," Miss Jennifer said. "Not that it was my fault that she got away. But I saw her last, and after a fashion she's my game."

Both Miss Rachel and Mayhew looked surprised at this bloodhound forcefulness on Miss Jennifer's part.

"We may move," Miss Rachel said as Mayhew showed signs of departure. "Ask at the grocery for our new location if we aren't here."

Mayhew nodded. "You won't be helping me if you get into trouble. Don't think I'm unappreciative of all you've done—I just don't like attending inquests on my friends. Be careful."

When he had gone and Miss Rachel had closed the front door after him, she returned to find Miss Jennifer sitting straight and watchful. "What," she asked, "is all this about our moving?"

Miss Rachel explained the woes of Mrs. Simpson and her own request to rent the tenant house of the Aldershots. While she talked she could see Jennifer's new-found instincts wavering.

"Isn't that where the crippled man hunts his spiders?" she asked. "I thought you said you'd even seen him there this morning."

"I did."

"I don't think that we'd better——"

Miss Rachel broke in: "Of course it will be ideal for you, too, in keeping a lookout for Florence. Depend on it, she'll find some way of getting in touch with whoever it is she hopes to get money from."

Doubt came into Miss Jennifer's eyes. "But I wasn't certain, Rachel. It was just a snatch out of all she said at the telephone. Maybe it isn't——"

Again Miss Rachel wouldn't let her finish. "How lucky you saw what she was wearing when she left and the direction in which she was walking. Why don't you start out after lunch and see if you can trace her from the village?"

The fervor returned gradually to Miss Jennifer's expression. "I could, couldn't I? She wouldn't have gone far in those high heels. Hmmmm. Do you know, Rachel, it's rather like hide and seek, isn't it?"

"But grimmer," Miss Rachel thought to herself. She felt a trickle of chill across her neck, remembering the first to hide in this particular game.

Tim Woodley. Counted *out*.

Miss Rachel awoke far in the middle of the night and lay listening to the unfamiliar creakings and stirrings of the Aldershot tenant house.

The room which she and Jennifer occupied was on the second floor. Its windows faced away from the valley, and from where she lay Miss Rachel could see the black bulk of San Cayetano shutting out the stars. The limbs of a tree made a pattern up one side of the pane, and when the tree moved with the wind there was the effect of spidery hands dawdling up and down the glass.

The rest of this upper floor was taken up with another bedroom—the use of which Jennifer had declined on the ground that there were now more important things than privacy—a large storeroom, a bath, and the stairs to the attic. The first floor contained a nondescript living room, a dinette, a large old-fashioned kitchen, and a pantry. The furniture, Miss Rachel suspected, was that discarded by the Aldershots when they had built their new home. It was worn and it was in the taste of the late nineteen-twenties.

Miss Jennifer was breathing placidly now in the dark, but before she had dropped off she had had a few things to say on the subject of people who went through life dragging other people into trouble with them. These remarks had not overly ruffled Miss Rachel. Miss Jennifer had been saying much the same since the time when she had been seven and Miss Rachel five and Miss Rachel had egged her into putting a frog into the church collection basket. Repetition had worn off the fine point of sarcasm. Miss Rachel smiled fondly now at the righteous angle of Miss Jennifer's nose, which she could see in outline in the faint light from the window.

Perhaps a part of Miss Jennifer's discomposure had been caused by her failure to trace Florence MacConnell. She had located Florence's car, still sitting in Mrs. Simpson's garage, but the trail of Florence's little high-heeled shoes vanished at the edge of the village.

The cat, sensing that Miss Rachel no longer slept, walked cautiously from the foot of the bed and stood just below Miss Rachel's shoulder and mewed. Obediently, and even a little glad of the chance to be up, Miss Rachel searched in the dark for slippers and robe and put them on. With the cat at her heels she felt her way into the unfamiliar hall and then stood still in a moment of confusion.

The house creaked and snapped as the wind pushed it, and the air of the hall was stuffy with the odors of ancient cooking and neglected cleanings. Miss Rachel felt her way toward what she believed to be the stairs.

She came instead to a door which, when opened, showed dimly the jumbled furnishings of the storeroom. An old wood heater in the center of the room with pipe attached reminded her of a closed fist with cocked, derisive thumb. A mirror on a side wall was like a pale face looking back at her. Miss Rachel shut the door hastily and went in the opposite direction.

Below she found the kitchen door and unlocked it, and while Samantha was out she breathed in the odor of orange trees and looked at the small moon and the multitude of stars.

It couldn't, she thought suddenly, be very far through the grove to the Aldershot home. There was a graveled path which had been put in, apparently for the convenience of whatever hired help might currently be occupying the tenant house. It appeared to lead away in a straight line. Without a second thought Miss Rachel pulled the door shut behind her, tucked her robe tight, and started off.

Samantha mewed in bewilderment and then decided to follow. The grove swallowed them in a tunnel of darkness. At its far end they came out into the clearing beside the Aldershot garages. A vigilant duck quacked in halfhearted alarm, and the pigeons stirred in their high cote. Samantha stopped; her green eyes regarded their quarters speculatively.

Miss Rachel caught her and spanked her gently and carried her as she circled the drive in the shelter of the trees.

There was no light showing, no sign of anyone about. The small moon made it possible to see the white bulk of the house, the dark tracery of grillwork, and the massed shadow of shrubbery. Miss Rachel walked cautiously as far as the drive that led off to the street, then cut across the lawn to make sure that no light shone where she and Jennifer had spied the night before.

The house was disappointingly dark and peaceful. The Aldershots slept, or else they had learned to get along without light in what they did. Not even by pressing her ear to a low pane could Miss Rachel make out any sign of life.

She decided to circle the house by going up its far side, and in doing so she almost came to disaster. Stakes had been set out and wires strung between them to bolster some now-vanished flowers, and Miss Rachel tripped on the wires and fell headlong.

She sat up as quickly as possible and listened to see whether her fall had roused anyone. Then she investigated her injuries.

She found a spot on her cheek grazed and stinging and a knee which she had wrenched in falling and which now throbbed in agony. Huddled inside the robe, she stifled an instinct to moan and took out the reaction to pain in rocking back and forth with her eyes shut.

Samantha came and rubbed briskly against her and purred as though this were some new sort of game in which she wished to join.

Just how long she sat in the dark nursing her knee Miss Rachel had no way of knowing. Nor did she know, or remotely guess, just how important that space of time was to be. When she rose at last and hobbled away the moon seemed to have dimmed and the breeze smelled faintly of dawn. There was no change in the black sky, the dark shoulder of the mountain like a watching giant.

She walked the graveled path in the grove slowly and painfully, conscious of chill and the lack of sleep. When she reached the kitchen door she found it unlatched and slightly ajar, but this could have been the result of her own previous inattention, and she gave it little heed. The cat followed her up the steps and into the hall that let into the bedrooms, and here a noticeably strange thing happened.

Out of the dark Samantha howled, a hoarse hollow sound that made Miss Rachel jump.

"Kitty, kitty!" she said softly and bent down.

The cat drew away and echoed the howl with a soft, querulous complaining deep in her throat.

Miss Rachel gave up trying to coax her. She opened the bedroom door and slid inside. She was instantly impaled in the beam from a flashlight.

"Rachel! Where on earth have you been? I've waited for you for hours!" Dimly, behind the light, Miss Jennifer could be seen inside a lump of bedding. "If you ever go away again I'll leave you here. I don't care what your excuse is. I won't endure this sort of thing."

"I've had Samantha out."

"All this long time?"

Miss Rachel thought guiltily to herself that perhaps the trip had consumed more time than she had thought. "I didn't realize—it's a lovely night outside."

"It isn't inside," Miss Jennifer snapped. "More creakings and squeakings—there must be rats in this house, Rachel. Huge things—you can hear them on the stairs. They fairly thump from one tread to another."

Slipping into bed, Miss Rachel wondered at Jennifer's positiveness about the rats. She hadn't noticed any scuttling retreat when she had gone out into the hall. And Jennifer was sure that she had heard them on the stairs, thumping from one tread to another.

And odd, too, she reflected sleepily, because the hall and the stairs were carpeted.

She awoke once more when dawn had made the sky milk-white and luminous; when every ridge, every meadow and crevasse on San Cayetano's heights was etched in purple and vermilion. Her drowsy senses had warned her that something was amiss. She looked half unseeingly at the mountain towering outside their windows, and it seemed that faint and far off there was a sound of something dripping.

She thought of the tap in the bathroom and went back to sleep.

CHAPTER XI

THEY WERE at breakfast in the rather dank and unattractive kitchen when, through a window that looked out toward the pathway in the grove, they saw a small man walking rapidly to the house.

"Mr. Krug," Miss Rachel decided, remembering the grass-hoppery silhouette in Mrs. Simpson's hall. "He's the manager over all the Aldershot properties. He tried to see Florence Mac-Connell the night before she disappeared."

Miss Jennifer peered disapprovingly through the curtains. "I never cared for that wiry type personally. They're always up to something."

Mr. Krug, after a moment's hesitation, came to knock at the kitchen door. With the morning sunlight behind him he looked innocent and small. "Ah—Miss Murdock, I presume? I'm Krug. I manage here. Miss Aldershot thought fit to wait until this morning before telling me you'd moved in. Somewhat irregular." He coughed deprecatingly. "Not that I should have disapproved. No, no. It's as well to get some return on the place, since it's not being used by the help. But—hurrrrph—you've found everything satisfactory?"

"Oh, quite." Miss Rachel stood aside. "Won't you come in?"

"Well, since you're good enough to ask me." He came in with a look of ill-concealed curiosity. He met Miss Jennifer's watchful gaze and bowed a trifle awkwardly. "Mmmmm—how do you do?"

"Good morning," Miss Jennifer said coolly.

"We were just having breakfast. Would you care to join us in a cup of coffee?" Miss Rachel made as if to take another cup from the cupboard.

"Oh no, thanks so much, but I couldn't. Upsets me. So sorry." But his narrow face rounded in a smile at her friendliness. "I just wanted to make sure that you were comfortable. Enough dishes and bedding and all that."

"Rats," said Miss Jennifer explosively, with a dark look at Miss Rachel.

"Not now, dear," Miss Rachel said sweetly, to Mr. Krug's evident bewilderment. "We were wondering about Miss MacConnell. Would she be apt to return here for something?"

His glance slid round the kitchen and then fixed itself on the toe of Miss Rachel's shoe. "Miss MacConnell? No, I shouldn't think she'd come here. Have you seen her?"

"Well—we weren't sure," Miss Rachel evaded. "We just thought, if some of the furnishings were hers——"

"Nothing," he cut in positively. "Absolutely nothing. I can't allow that sort of thing. If you'll tell me her present address I'll speak to her about it."

"Oh, I wouldn't care to cause her any trouble."

"We can't have any molestation of the tenants." Mr. Krug drew his little height into pomposity. "If she said where she's staying I'll see that nothing like that happens again."

Miss Rachel glanced at Miss Jennifer to see if she had caught

Mr. Krug's anxiety to locate Florence. Miss Jennifer was looking glumly at the lower cupboards, as if speculating when the rats would begin jumping out of them.

"You mustn't worry about us," Miss Rachel said simperingly.

Mr. Krug simpered back, but his eyes were gimlets. "There are other—hurrrrph—matters I should like to take up with Florence. Miss MacConnell, that is. If you'll just tell me where she is."

"She's really Mrs. Aldershot, you know," Miss Jennifer put in unexpectedly.

"Yes." Blank surprise settled over him that they should know, but briefly. "Yes. So it is said. Most unlike Robert to have acted secretly in this." He stood quiet, looking at them. The conversation seemed to have reached an impasse.

Miss Jennifer fidgeted, and a look came over her as though she were about to blurt out something. To forestall any calamitous utterances Miss Rachel stammered: "Is there something more? Would you like"—her thoughts raced—"would you like to look through the house, to check up, perhaps?"

Mr. Krug seemed to give up thinking about Robert's perfidy. "Yes, I might. It's usual with renting, isn't it? And you won't mind?"

"Not at all." Miss Rachel moved to usher him into the lower hall, where doors let into living room and dinette and where the stairs went up to the second floor. "Shall I show you? Or would you rather check through by yourself?"

He stood in doubt, his resemblance to a bug heightened by the gloom of the hall and the fact that by looking in one direction and another he seemed to be trying out a pair of feelers. "I don't wish to interrupt your breakfast. Suppose I glance into the rooms very quickly and make a mental note of things as I go?"

"That will be all right. We didn't bring any furnishings, just our personal things. They're all in the north bedroom."

He bowed. "Just routine. I shouldn't bother with it, except that I have a sort of responsibility to the estate. Goes with the job, you know." Hesitantly he went to the dinette and peered in.

Miss Rachel discreetly left him. She found Miss Jennifer making fresh toast in the oven. "What's he doing?" Miss Jennifer asked.

"He's satisfying his curiosity about us, I suppose." Miss Rachel plied the toast with butter. "He's very curious about everyone, isn't he?"

"Florence MacConnell in particular," Miss Jennifer said, proving that she hadn't missed anything.

"I wish I could think of some way to ask him what he wanted of Florence, when he called at Mrs. Simpson's that evening."

"And whether it was he she talked with while I listened."

"Hmmmm."

"And still, she went away as though she'd made some sort of arrangement through that call. If she's blackmailing Mr. Krug he shouldn't be so anxious to get hold of her, and he should know where she is."

"He may be putting on an act," Miss Rachel decided. "I'm going to try to think up some innocent-sounding question to trip him."

She was still trying to think of the question when Mr. Krug returned. He came into the kitchen quite precipitously and would have made for the door in a straight line if Miss Rachel hadn't risen to detain him.

"Through so soon?" she asked.

He wiped his forehead with a handkerchief from his coat pocket, as though the trip up- and downstairs had tired him.

"Yes. Quite finished. I've remembered—hurrrrph—just remembered something I forgot to do. Must hurry." He put his hand on the knob.

It was now or never, and Miss Rachel could think of no way to get out of him by subterfuge what she wished to know. So she said boldly, "I believe it was you, Mr. Krug, who came searching for Florence MacConnell at Mrs. Simpson's house. Wasn't it?"

He looked at her oddly without saying a word, as if, Miss Rachel thought, there were some horrible and inexplicable meaning behind her question.

"I?" he got out when the silence had become noticeable. "I, at Mrs. Simpson's?"

"I thought if you would tell me what it was you wanted of Florence that I could mention it when I saw her." It was weak; Miss Rachel had little hope that he would come out baldly with his motive in looking for the girl. But she was scarcely prepared for the effect on Mr. Krug.

He shook his head violently. "You've made a grievous error, Miss Murdock. Quite grievous." He tried to smile and could not and stood clinging to the knob, limp and ghastly. "I've never been in the least interested in Miss MacConnell's whereabouts. I wouldn't have any reason to be asking for her anywhere. My contacts with her were in the strictest sense businesslike. Please don't repeat this statement of yours, Miss Murdock. I beg you."

He had the door open. Popeyed, a trifle lonely-looking, he hurried away.

"What on earth," Miss Jennifer wondered, "got into him all of a sudden?"

"I suppose I frightened him with the blunt question. Still, he hadn't been exactly shy in asking where we thought Florence was. He's had a change of heart about trying to find her."

"Decidedly." Miss Jennifer's attention was drawn again to the window. "Here's someone else, and he's coming here. Rachel." She rose from the table to put her face against the curtain. "It's that rude young man Miss Aldershot met in the driveway. He's—yes, he's going to knock at the door. What shall we do?"

"Let him in," Miss Rachel said. "And find out, if we can, who *he's* looking for."

But, oddly, Tommy Hale didn't knock. He walked to the kitchen door and tried the knob, and since Miss Rachel had, without thinking, snapped the night latch in place after Mr. Krug's departure, the door didn't open. Tommy Hale said something under his breath; they heard his steps go up the walk beside the house and then, a minute later, the brisk rattle of the front-door lock.

"He is rude!" Miss Jennifer cried. "He's trying to walk in on us. After all, even if we are just renters, he's only the help." She stood in the middle of the kitchen, listened to Tommy's efforts at the front door in outrage.

"He doesn't know we're here," Miss Rachel said suddenly. "Of course! Quick, Jennifer. Get out of sight. The broom closet." She pushed Miss Jennifer ahead of her into the narrow space, pulled the door almost shut. The dry and dirty tendrils of a hanging mop made a fringe over Miss Jennifer's forehead, and her usually neat white ruffles were bunched beneath her chin like the feathers of a sick fowl. Miss Rachel felt a pang of pity. Then she was all ears and as still as a mouse, for Tommy Hale was climbing in at a window in the dinette.

The odor of their breakfast may have drawn him, for he came first to the kitchen. He must have stood looking at their table for a long while; there was no movement and no sound out of him.

Then he turned and went out. Presently the stairs creaked on the other side of the wall.

"Rats! There they are again!" Miss Jennifer said. "And in daylight too. Rachel, if they're that bold, if they'll come out any time——"

Miss Rachel was looking at her oddly. "That noise isn't rats, Jennifer. It's Tommy Hale going upstairs."

"Sounds the same," Miss Jennifer complained, subsiding under the mop fringe.

"He's going toward our bedroom!" Miss Rachel whispered. "Be quiet, Jennifer. Don't even breathe!"

"I can't anyway." Then Miss Jennifer, to disprove her statement, drew her breath in sharply and paused, eyes squeezed shut and mouth open.

"Don't *sneeze!*"

The sneeze was explosive and catapulted Miss Jennifer out of the broom closet, accompanied by the mop and Miss Rachel. They were picking themselves up when a step came in the doorway and Tommy Hale stood there soberly, looking at them.

"I'm sorry if I disturbed you. I didn't realize there was anyone living here." His angular face ("he's good-looking in his way," Miss Jennifer was thinking) professed the right degree of regret. "You must have moved in yesterday. I was working the other end of the grove and so missed seeing you. Please excuse me."

"Certainly. There's no harm done. We thought you were a burglar, so we hid." Miss Rachel, quickly composed, put the fallen articles back into the broom closet and shut the door. "We've heard such queer sounds since we've moved into this house. Thumps and bumps and creakings. So we were somewhat jumpy to begin with."

She was watching him over her shoulder. His young face with

its half-ironic smile had turned grim and sober, and his eyes were on the battered work hat in his hands. "Have you any idea of what makes these sounds?"

"I have," Miss Jennifer said. "And if our cat weren't such a lazy old tabby she'd get busy and clear them out."

"Rats?" He glanced at Miss Jennifer with a trace of surprise.

"What do *you* suppose causes them?" Miss Rachel put in.

"I don't know." A veiled, unhappy look had come into his face. "Perhaps someone else who doesn't know the house is occupied. A tramp, maybe." He shrugged.

"I suggested to Mr. Krug that the former tenants might have returned for something they forgot."

He looked up, alert. "What did he say?"

"He said that it was quite impossible."

"No, he didn't, Rachel," Miss Jennifer corrected. "He said that if we'd tell him where Florence MacConnell—or Aldershot; I keep forgetting—*was,* he'd go to her and make sure that it didn't happen again." She paused. "I still say that it's rats."

"Did you tell him where Florence was?" Tommy Hale asked quickly.

"We didn't know." Miss Rachel seemed mildly regretful. "Do you?"

Some flicker of unease showed in his eyes. "No. Not any more."

"Have you seen her since she left Mrs. Simpson's?"

He appeared to think over his answer before he gave it. "No. She called me yesterday at about noon to say that she was leaving but that she'd see me before long."

Miss Jennifer choked. "Then it was you!"

He looked at her warily and said nothing. Miss Rachel's little motion, begging Jennifer not to go on, went unnoticed.

"It was *you* she was blackmailing!"

He had become as still as stone. A knot of muscle bulged in his chin and then relaxed. His eyes studied Miss Jennifer as though she were some new, uncounted-upon element in a serious game. "I don't believe I know just what you mean. Is Florence in some sort of trouble?"

But Miss Rachel forestalled Jennifer's answer. "You said Florence had called you. Do you mean by phone from Mrs. Simpson's?"

"No." He measured Miss Rachel in her turn. "She said she was in the village store. I gathered she had already left Mrs. Simpson's and was on her way somewhere else."

"Did she say where?"

He shook his head. "I didn't ask her."

"Did you come here this morning thinking she might be here?"

He seemed to decide suddenly to be frank. "Yes, I did. I knew the place was still furnished and I had a hunch that Florence might want to stay in the neighborhood. She's married to Mr. Aldershot, you know." He turned back to Miss Jennifer. "I don't understand what you meant by 'blackmailing.' Why should Florence be blackmailing anyone?"

Miss Rachel developed a certain coyness. "Nobody knows. Jennifer just heard a snatch of what Miss MacConnell said on the phone. It wasn't eavesdropping," she explained carefully to Miss Jennifer's gratification. "The phone is in the hall at Mrs. Simpson's, and you can't help hearing sometimes."

He brushed all this away with an impatient gesture. "I'm sure she wasn't eavesdropping. But what was it Florence said?"

Miss Jennifer had been watching her sister. She, too, now had a mysterious reticence. "I don't recall the words. Just a hint of trying to get money out of someone."

"Money?" He said the word slowly and then laughed. Miss Rachel thought that he looked suddenly relieved. It was true that any blackmail involving money might be presumed to let him out.

Still, as she pointed out to Miss Jennifer after Tommy Hale had gone, there were other facts to be considered. When Jeff Woodley had suggested that his dead brother might have known of Florence being indiscreet, Tommy had wanted to know in a hurry if Tim had seen her with anybody. That suggested, somehow, a rendezvous.

"And that song Florence was singing as I passed her," Miss Jennifer said. "I can't forget it, nor the spiteful, triumphant way she hummed it. If a cat could sing, that's just the way she'd sound."

"Don't malign the cat family," Miss Rachel said. She was absent-mindedly watching Samantha, who sat washing her fur in a square of noonday sun under the livingroom window. "But why should Florence have been singing 'I Can't Give You Anything but Love'?"

CHAPTER XII

IT WAS early afternoon when Miss Jennifer looked out of the kitchen door to find Reuben Carder watching her from his wheel chair.

"Oh," she said. "How do you do?"

"Well, thanks." He put strong hands on the wheels and brought himself closer. "Krug told me a short while ago about your moving in. Sorry I wasn't on hand earlier to greet you."

"Nasty grin he's got," Miss Jennifer thought.

"You've found everything quite satisfactory, I hope. No trouble with lights or heat? Good. Don't mind the stillness. You're quite a way from town, you know."

"I don't mind it," Miss Jennifer said, trying not to sound too frosty.

He had reached into a little basket on his lap and brought forth a capped jar. "I have the most beautiful specimen here, best I've caught in months. I found him under the trellis at the back of your house. Would you like to see him?"

Miss Jennifer ventured out upon the graveled drive. Inside the jar was a yellow-and-black spider who seemed to watch her malevolently. His long legs tested the glass, as though searching for freedom.

"I've literally millions of these things inside my spider hut," Mr. Carder went on. The little white mustache twisted with his smile. "Would you like to see them? Your sister too, perhaps?"

"Heavens," Miss Jennifer said, "if it's spiders you've got——"

"We'd love to see them," Miss Rachel finished behind her. Miss Jennifer jumped around. Miss Rachel, carrying the cat, had come up very quietly. "Mr. Carder, I don't believe you've met my sister. Jennifer, this is Miss Aldershot's uncle."

Miss Jennifer was about to say she'd recognized him from Miss Rachel's description and then decided not to. She just smiled.

"Miss Murdock," he murmured, inclining his head as if to bow. "Yes, I'd guessed so, from what Mr. Krug told me. Should have introduced myself. Getting careless. Bad habit, slighting the formalities. However—will you see my spider collection?"

"I'm looking forward to it," Miss Rachel answered. She frowned at Jennifer, who had begun shaking her head as soon as Carder had turned in his chair to lead them. "It must be an interesting hobby, collecting them. Though not easy"—she was watching the back of Mr. Carder's head—"in your position."

His ears had the look of listening. It was an instant before he said: "I'm not as helpless as you may suppose. I tire easily, and the chair is necessary because I have to move about somewhat to supervise the work here. But I'm not bound to it."

"He's saying that," Miss Jennifer thought, "because he knows I'm looking at the trellis and remembering that he said he'd caught this spider there."

The trellis was high, fairly covered with dried vines, and would have been out of Carder's reach from the wheel chair. They passed it as Carder led the way along a dirt track that led off at an angle from the graveled pathway to the Aldershot home. The trees closed in behind them to make a green tunnel; coolness came up from the earth, and the sky seemed farther and less blue. Miss Jennifer turned imploring eyes to her sister.

But Miss Rachel was looking ahead, where a brown door showed suddenly between two trees, as though it had been conjured there. The weathered boards showed traces of moss, and a little creeping growth had spread at the bottom, as though the shed had taken root and had started to grow. Carder took hold of the brown earthenware knob and pulled the door outward.

"'Will you come into my parlor?'" he quoted sardonically. "That's my stock line to new visitors. You'll have to forgive me. It always seemed so appropriate."

They went ahead of him into greener, darker gloom.

It was, somehow, like being under water. At either side a big pane let in grayish light, and spattered on the glass in designs resembling seaweed were the dark wiggling bodies of Mr. Carder's collected pets. The aisle in which they stood was without illumination except from the web-filled enclosures beyond the glass. Miss Rachel suspected that skylights above these spaces accounted for the underwater illusion. Being here was like being submerged into nightmare.

The designs made by the circular legs, millions of them, broke and reformed constantly in some places, remained static in others. These latter spots, where immobile horrors etched their shapes against the pane in an attitude suggestive of hungry waiting, caused Miss Jennifer to start shivering.

"Chilly, isn't it?" she asked Mr. Carder, who was watching. "I don't suppose it's necessary to keep them warm, though. Spiders can live anywhere, can't they?"

"Almost." There was spiderish stillness in the way he looked at the two of them. "I can't say, however, that I've given them really scientific study. I enjoy seeing their coloring—it's often quite striking and beautiful. Their cruelty, their agility and cleverness are almost past belief. This"—he motioned toward the glassed-in spaces—"is a sort of dog-eat-dog arrangement. They live off each other, you see. Some species are cannibalistic. Some apparently aren't."

Miss Jennifer's gulp was loud in the utter quiet.

"When I feel that they've been sufficiently cannibalistic," he went on, "I clear out a lot and let the pigeons have them."

It seemed to Miss Jennifer that Rachel's face swam between her and the spotted pane and spoke. But Miss Jennifer was too busy fighting off a sick feeling to listen.

"We'll come again. Jennifer doesn't seem to be well," Miss Rachel was saying. She saw the mocking stare—Carder's eyes were as watchful, as fixed, as one of the things against the glass—and she resented it. Poor Jennifer! Carder had had a good time with her. Jennifer's skin matched the whiteness of her little knob of hair, and her lips had turned positively purple.

"Come any time you feel like it," he said. "Don't mind if I'm not around. Perhaps, though, I should warn you." He paused on a note of deliberation that Miss Rachel knew to be utterly false. "Sometimes—not often—a few find a way to escape. And it's possible those few might be deadly."

Miss Jennifer was outside now, swallowing air and straining to get away. She had no words for Mr. Carder.

But Miss Rachel was sterner stuff. She looked at the white-haired man in the doorway. The panes behind him seemed to converge, to make a wedge of scampering horror from which his face peered, brown and scornful. "Good afternoon," she said simply. "I think we understand each other."

Back inside the tenant house, Miss Jennifer sank down into a kitchen chair and shut her eyes. "Never, Rachel, did I think we'd come to this. That hideous man. The way he talked to us."

"He was trying to frighten us." Miss Rachel brought Miss Jennifer a cool drink from the tap. "I wonder why?"

"Do you think that Monica Aldershot bothered to tell *anybody* we'd moved in here?"

"Her brother, perhaps. No one else, from what they've told us. She may, of course, be a very thoughtless person. Or a very shrewd one. I think she let us move in here and kept it secret deliberately. Perhaps she thought we'd catch her—her *rats*—for her."

Miss Jennifer's eyes flew wide open. "How peculiarly you said that, Rachel! Almost as though you didn't believe—— But of course it *was* rats." She waited, sipping the water. "Wasn't it?"

"I never knew a rat to walk just like a man," Miss Rachel answered. "And that's how your rats sounded. Just like Tommy Hale going upstairs."

"They must be large ones."

"And two-legged."

Silence came between them: two little Dresden figures in taffeta looking at each other in fear and surmise.

"I think that I'll have a glance into the rooms upstairs," Miss Rachel decided. "Stay here, Jennifer. And you might lock the doors, just in case."

Halfway up the stairs Miss Rachel turned to find Miss Jennifer creeping after her. Miss Jennifer stopped guiltily, then came slowly on. Miss Rachel sighed. Jennifer was looking over her shoulder when she opened the door of the storeroom.

The collected and outmoded stuff—old dressers, broken chairs, whatnots, and bric-a-brac—gave the impression of a forgotten junk shop. The north light made it bleak. Against the left wall, the stove with its attached pipe looked peculiarly cold.

Miss Rachel was about to shut the door when some prodding memory, some ghost of unease made her look again. There was something wrong here, something amiss or changed or out of place. For a long moment she stood in the door, feeling Jennifer's frightened breath on her shoulder, hearing the vague noises made by the old house in the rising wind.

It was, she thought, something about the stove. She tried to remember the room as she had seen it the night before. The stove had seemed to make a columnar mark against the windows, where now it stood at the side of the room.

She walked toward it, finding a path between the grouped furnishings without any difficulty. The stove was a small wood-burning heater, not of cast iron, as she had at first supposed, but of thin stamped-out sheets. A touch set it rattling, set the pipe wobbling; a little sprinkling of soot came down to rest on her gray taffeta sleeve. Beneath the stove was a metal-and-felt mat, some three feet square, intended to protect the floor when the fire was burning.

She went to the center of the room. Here was an empty space in which the stove had at one time stood. Blobs of soot outlined the shape of the mat, and in the direction of the left wall the blobs were pulled out into streaks where the mat had been drawn across them.

Miss Jennifer's eyes were big. "What is it, Rachel? Did you find anything?"

"I don't know," Miss Rachel admitted. "The stove seems to have been moved, and from my memory of the room last night, I'd say that the moving was very recent. But I can't be sure. And what could it mean, anyway?"

The cat walked in and stood switching her tail, as though something displeased her. Where the stove had stood she gave the floor a cautious sniffing. At the edge of the metal floor mat she paused to emit dolorous yowls, then got out fast.

"I wish we'd never come here," Miss Jennifer whispered. "I don't like the atmosphere of this place. The silence, the sense of waiting is exactly the same as it is in Mr. Carder's spider house. I feel as though there were something poised over us"—her eyes rose to the ceiling as if in search of menace—"over us, and it's——" Her voice died. Mouth and eyes made Os of horror.

But while Miss Jennifer had made her discovery upon the ceiling of the storeroom Miss Rachel had skipped to the door and now stood there listening.

"I heard a step downstairs. I'm sure of it. A quiet step, Jennifer. We seem to have most peculiar callers. They never knock. They simply slip in and prowl."

Miss Jennifer, torn between two terrors, fled after Miss Rachel to the head of the stairs. After all, a prowler was alive, whereas the thing on the ceiling . . . She clutched the banister with a hand that shook and watched Miss Rachel slip down step by step like a bird with its eye on a pile of crumbs.

Suddenly—so suddenly that Miss Jennifer gave a little cry and all but fell off the top stair—Monica Aldershot came into view and stood in the lower hall, looking up at them.

"Hello! Hope I didn't startle you. It's so gloomy in here I wasn't even sure who it was at first."

"Hello." Miss Rachel went down quickly with composure that

Miss Jennifer envied. "I was hoping you'd come by. We owe you at least a cup of tea for letting us move in."

"Is everything comfortable?"

"Oh, quite comfortable, thanks." She looked at Monica and marveled again at the clear beauty—the sulky, arresting eyes, the frosty lips—and wondered if, after all, there might be an incredible cruelty behind them. Had it been Monica in the long swooping car; had Monica's lovely face looked through the windshield at Tim Woodley's hurtling, helpless body? Could it have been Monica who beat the unconscious man to death, covered him hurriedly with dirt in the Los Angeles River bottom?

And if so—and more baffling—*why?*

Miss Rachel had led the way into the kitchen, where she put on a kettle and lit the gas. Monica followed. She was dressed carelessly in a tweed skirt and red jacket whose well-worn appearance couldn't hide the fact that they were exquisitely cut and fitted. She sat down on a kitchen chair and drew an idle pattern on the kitchen linoleum with the toe of her oxford.

"I don't suppose you've found out anything," she said suddenly.

Miss Rachel paused, arrested in the act of taking down the tea.

"About Florence," Monica continued, as though not noticing Miss Rachel's action. "She's disappeared, you know. My brother's very angry. She's acted peculiarly in this whole affair. If she has reasons for her behavior she'd better bring them forward."

"Your brother thinks," Miss Rachel said, "that she deliberately lured him away as a part of this plot you mentioned?"

Monica nodded. "And Tim, you see, being the faithful old fellow he was, went up to warn Robert. And was murdered for it." Some of the color left her face; the frosty lips grew tight. "That's why Robert must find her. She obviously knows the whole story, was a party to whatever rotten scheme was being hatched."

"Why is your brother so sure," Miss Rachel wondered, "that there *was* a plot? Why couldn't it have been some simple but important fact that Woodley had discovered, which he felt your brother should know? He was killed to keep it secret. Wouldn't that be as reasonable?"

"I don't quite see what you mean," Monica answered. "Wouldn't that in itself be a plot?"

Miss Rachel's thoughts had been busy with the fact that Woodley must have known of some indiscretion on Florence's part and that young Tommy Hale's attitude suggested that the indiscretion had been with him. Suppose Woodley had finally decided to go to Robert with what he knew, and Tommy, having now a determination to punish Monica for her family's scorn of him in addition to a liking for her money, had killed Woodley to keep this absolutely fatal information from leaking out? Monica's fierce pride would have made any dallying with Florence a cause for a complete breakup; whereas, as things were, Miss Rachel suspected that Monica's real feeling for Tommy was one of sympathy and conciliation, in spite of her surface showing of anger and spite, and that Tommy knew it.

All this went through her mind while she looked into Monica's questioning green eyes. She wished suddenly that there was a way of lifting up Monica's pale hair and of seeing exactly what was under it. A brain was, of course. Was it a brain in which guilt and ferocity mingled?

Miss Jennifer came tottering in through the kitchen doorway, and it struck Miss Rachel that Jennifer hadn't acted quite right since the two of them had been in the storeroom. The oddity of the stove that seemed to have moved of itself, Jennifer's story of the rats, her imploring glance at the ceiling . . .

Miss Jennifer crept to a chair and sat down in it.

Monica was watching curiously. "Is something wrong, Miss Murdock?"

Miss Jennifer opened her eyes gradually, as though afraid of seeing something she didn't wish to. "Up there," she whispered hoarsely. *"Blood. It's made a horrible big spot on the storeroom wall-paper."*

CHAPTER XIII

THE SILENCE that came after Miss Jennifer's remark reminded Miss Rachel of the scene in *Hands of Darkness* where a gorilla's paw slid through a curtain to hover over the innocent head of the heroine. There was the same sense of breathless dread, of wanting to scream, and of not wanting to miss anything that might come afterward—only this was real; Miss Jennifer, with her terrified eyes, was there in the flesh, and Monica's voice was drawlingly non-committal.

"It must be just a rain stain," Monica said. "The roof's so old, I wouldn't be surprised if it leaked like a sieve."

Miss Rachel shook herself out of the reverie over *Hands of Darkness,* a remarkably good movie, and said, "Let's go see."

"You can go. I mean one of you can go," Miss Jennifer answered. "I'm not going to budge out of the kitchen, and I insist that one of you stay here with me. I'm afraid. I don't mind admitting it."

Monica raised her eyebrows a little, the lovely eyebrows which she had dyed beautifully because they unfortunately matched her platinum hair. "Of course. We'll stay with you. It isn't anything, anyway. What could it be?"

"There is no doubt something in the attic," Miss Jennifer said with dreadful distinctness, "which has leaked down and made a spot on the storeroom ceiling. I don't mean rain."

Miss Rachel's eyes in their turn grew big. "I remember—that dripping sound. Last night, after I'd come back from"—she hesitated, took care not to glance at Monica with any show of guilt—"from the bathroom," she went on meaningly to Miss Jennifer. "And I thought I'd left the basin tap open. Except that now, come to think of it, the sound wasn't the same as a tap dripping. There was a woodeny note to it. Like rain falling through upon a floor."

"It wasn't raining," Miss Jennifer pointed out.

"No. It wasn't. So I think we'd just better see what there is in the attic."

Monica said, "I'm not going to let you go up there alone," and so Miss Jennifer had to follow or be left by herself. They made a procession of shadows on the stairs; in the upper hall they paused to look at each other. Monica was smiling with a show of amusement, but it was forced. Miss Rachel looked grave, and Miss Jennifer was shivering.

"I'll go up first." Miss Rachel opened the door to the attic stairs and put a foot on the lowest tread. A faint creaking followed.

"That's it," Miss Jennifer whispered. "It's the sound I thought was made by rats."

"You haven't checked this so-called spot on the ceiling," Monica said suddenly. "I'll have a look at it." She took three steps and stopped in the door of the room beyond the stairway. From the opening of the stairs Miss Rachel could see the change in her. The amusement, the youthful insulation against shock went out of her on an ebb of color. She came back pale and quiet. "It's there. It's—just what Miss Jennifer says it is."

They went up a tunnel of gloom and emerged into the cobwebbed silence of the attic. A low dirty window at either end of the gabled space gave a little light. Monica took a match from her jacket pocket—"I brought a few from the kitchen," she explained—and began a search through the clutter of stored and broken furnishings.

This attic and the storeroom below had evidently received the cast-off belongings of the Aldershots for a considerable time. Here the furnishings were older, dustier, farther past repair. The Aldershots, Miss Rachel reflected, needed a housecleaning in more ways than one. An ancient cylinder-type phonograph swayed on its stand as she brushed it; the big horn swung round with a screech, and Miss Jennifer whimpered.

The yellow cone of flame in Monica's hand had steadied itself near the left wall. Miss Rachel, peering across a broken bookcase, saw a huddle of clothing on the floor, a wide sticky puddle that shone dully in the glare, a white hand flung out as if to clutch at something, and a smart little hat, bedraggled now with dust.

She knew the hat the instant she saw it. It had been perched on Florence MacConnell's head when she had looked at them from Mrs. Simpson's upper window.

Monica bent down slowly and pulled at the shoulder of the girl on the floor. Even Miss Rachel could see the rigid resistance of the body under Monica's touch.

"She's—stiff," Monica said. She raised a sick face to Miss Rachel's. "She's been dead a long while, hasn't she?"

Miss Jennifer went down the stairs quickly, and then it was utterly quiet. In the still yellow glow from the dying match Monica looked at the things that lay near the body.

There was a suitcase with the lid thrown back and a froth of expensive lingerie spilling out incongruously beside a thermos bottle and a half-eaten sandwich on a paper plate. The girl's purse lay beside the suitcase; it had been torn inside out, the heaped contents—lipstick, compact, mirror, comb, handkerchief, scraps of paper, and a scattering of change—put beside it. And, running beneath all of it, like a river at flood, was the congealing stain of Florence MacConnell's blood.

The match went out, and in the little well of darkness beside Florence's body Monica's voice said, "She's cut her throat. I never saw anything so ghastly."

"Light another match," Miss Rachel said.

In the renewed yellow light Miss Rachel bent over the body. From Florence's clenched hand she pulled forth a torn bit of paper, heavy paper marked with green, and examined it closely.

"That's money," Monica whispered.

Miss Rachel smoothed the scrap against her palm. Uppermost was the figure that marked it as a hundred-dollar bill. Though she didn't tell Monica, the thought occurred to her that this was the stuff for which Florence had died. Even in her death agonies, with her life's blood going out like a tide, Florence had clung leech-like to it.

"I think we'd better call your local officers," Miss Rachel decided. "And perhaps I'd better call Lieutenant Mayhew too," she added silently to herself. "He'll forgive me then, surely, for the trick I played in getting up here before he did."

Before going she looked about carefully, trying to fix in her mind the position of the objects on the floor. A scattering of cigarette ends, matches, and the half-eaten lunch spoke of a long vigil on Florence's part. She must have been up here, Miss Rachel thought suddenly, all of the while that she and Miss Jennifer had been moving in, getting settled, unpacking, and going finally to bed. She had sat here in the gloom of the attic, waiting, wondering, perhaps, if the occupants below would prevent the rendezvous she wanted.

And outside someone else must have waited, perhaps even more impatiently than Florence, for a chance to slip in and do what must be done. Miss Rachel's midnight prowl, her long absence because of the hurt to her knee had been the chance they both had waited for. Florence had got the money she had demanded. Her visitor had given or shown it to her in an effort, perhaps, to throw her off guard. There had been quick work, then. Murderous work.

For it was murder. The straight-edged razor which had obviously done the job of cutting Florence's throat had been put carefully on top of the bookcase; beside it lay the thing with which it had been cleaned—a satin brassière which matched the creamy froth from Florence's suitcase. A breath of heather sachet stole from the underthings to mingle with the stuffiness of the attic, a breath out of the past of this girl who had loved luxury and riches.

"I can't——" Monica said in a strangled voice. "I've got to get out." She stumbled away toward the stairs.

Miss Rachel lit one more match, the last of three she had taken from Monica. She bent over the sprawled, still form. The dark hair gave forth a reddish glint; the skin was waxen, drained. On the outflung hand she saw a new detail—a wedding ring, obviously cheap. There was something suddenly pitiful about the dead, clutching hand. It had tried to grasp so much—too much. In one scoop it had gathered marriage, wealth, respectability— and then gone on to try to wring more money from some dark knowledge. Why, Miss Rachel wondered, hadn't Florence Mac-

Connell let well enough alone, been satisfied with her marriage to an Aldershot?

She was still puzzling over the contradictions in the girl's behavior when Mayhew arrived on the heels of the local officers.

Mayhew stopped with them briefly in the living room. "I suggest that all of you wait with Miss Aldershot at her home." He looked at Monica; she nodded agreement. "We'll be busy here for some time. Don't discuss what you've seen with anyone, nor compare notes with each other. I want individual, fresh viewpoints. Try to rest, and don't have hysterics, please."

Miss Jennifer, who had contracted hiccups in the midst of the excitement, blinked guiltily. She tried holding her breath and counting to fifty.

"Meanwhile, jot down any small details you can recall—things that you might forget later. I'll see you as quickly as I can."

He went away, big and brown and impressive, and they heard his thumping steps go up into the higher reaches of the old house.

"Let's go, then." Monica stood up. "I'll have the housekeeper make us a pot of tea. Personally, I think we need a——" Her eyes took in Miss Jennifer's acid primness. "No, on second thought we'll do with the tea."

The shadow of San Cayetano made the pathway through the grove chilly and gloomy; a surf of clouds beyond the summit gave an unseasonable look of rain. Miss Rachel caught up with Monica when Miss Jennifer paused to pick up the cat.

"You were saying——" Monica looked blank. "About the tea, you know," Miss Rachel went on. "If you'd lace it with a bit of spirits Jennifer won't know. She's unfamiliar with liquor. And I agree with you—I'm sure you were about to say it—that a little lift wouldn't do us any harm."

So they sat in Monica's little sanctum, a room which combined adolescent athletic prizes with *Vogue,* philosophy, and a little collection of rare china, and drank tea laced with scotch. It was good scotch, and Miss Jennifer decided that a third cup wouldn't be too much. She fell fast asleep while Miss Rachel and Monica, each with a slip of paper and a pencil and a book to write on, jotted down their memories of the thing in the tenant-house attic.

Miss Rachel's paper went this way:

The last sight I had of Florence MacConnell alive was yesterday at about noon. She was standing in an upper room of Mrs. Simpson's house looking out at us. She got out by means of the back stairway before Monica could talk to her.

Previously Jennifer had overheard two sentences from a telephone conversation which might mean that Florence was trying to blackmail someone. (I'll let Jennifer write about this.) After her disappearance from Mrs. Simpson's house Florence passed Jennifer in the village. Florence was singing "I Can't Give You Anything but Love, Baby."

From the evidence surrounding the body—a great many cigarettes, the remains of a meal—I conclude that Florence must have come to the tenant house almost directly from Mrs. Simpson's. Since Jennifer didn't overhear any mention of the tenant house by Florence in the telephone conversation, it may mean that the rendezvous was set by the other person. Getting Florence into the supposedly vacant tenant house would serve two purposes. It would keep her out of reach of the police, for questioning, and make murdering her much easier.

Jennifer and I moved in during the afternoon, and Florence must have heard us—but she made no move to leave and did not betray her presence. Evidently the rendezvous was so important to her she dared not miss keeping it by getting away.

At sometime about midnight (I'm guessing at the time, but it seemed sort of middle-of-the-night-y) I awoke and went down to let the cat out. A whim took me to walk through the grove to the Aldershot house. On this walk I stumbled and fell and hurt my knee so badly I had to sit awhile until the pain went away. When I returned Jennifer complained that she had been kept awake by terrific activity on the part of "rats." (I wonder, by the way, if I should have been murdered if I had come in at the wrong time: when the murderer was leaving, for instance? Jennifer's staying quiet in bed undoubtedly saved her from a fate exactly like Florence's.)

Thinking back upon what might have happened, three gruesome killings instead of one, made Miss Rachel feel sick and shivery. She looked at Monica, pale and sober, writing slowly on her own paper across the room.

I woke a long while after coming back and heard a dripping noise.

But wait. The seepage from the attic through upon the ceiling of the storeroom wouldn't have made a dripping noise. Besides, as she had told Miss Jennifer, it had had the sound of rain falling through—falling a long way, to strike drop by drop upon a floor.

A floor—the floor of the storeroom!

It all raced through her mind in a series of pictures as vivid as daylight. Mr. Krug going up coolly to inspect the upper rooms; Mr. Krug all but falling over himself getting out. He'd been in the storeroom, of course; he'd seen a puddle of blood on the floor; he'd moved the stove and the stove mat to cover it. And then raced away—*where?*

"You've got to get hold of Mr. Krug!" Miss Rachel cried, springing up. "You see, it must have been he who moved the stove; he must know everything—whom Florence meant to see, who followed her there, whom she had been blackmailing. . . ."

Monica had raised her face in astonishment. And Miss Rachel, abashed, had blushed crimson.

For Mr. Krug, a bedraggled, wet-sparrow Mr. Krug, stood in the doorway looking in at her.

CHAPTER XIV

"No, no, no," Mr. Krug said weakly. "I mean I don't know the least about all that you've mentioned. I moved the stove, yes. I confess doing that in a moment of panic—sheer unreasoning horror. I thought to save you ladies from a shock. You see, I ran across Florence's body in the attic—I began by inspecting the attic this morning—and it upset me so, I wasn't quite as reasonable and logical as I might have been otherwise. I just covered up the bloodstains on the floor of the storeroom so that you and your sister wouldn't see them." He stopped and gulped loudly.

"And left us there in the house with the corpse," Miss Rachel said sweetly. "I appreciate your thoughtfulness, Mr. Krug."

He waggled his hands helplessly, like a bird with two broken wings. "I was stupid, I know. I've been thinking since, trying to figure out a way to get you ladies out before poor Florence's body was discovered."

"Weren't you a little guilty about concealing a murder, Mr. Krug?"

"Murder?" He wrinkled his high, bare forehead. "Not murder, surely. Poor Florence killed herself. She'd had such a hectic, un- settled life, poor girl, and she——"

"She didn't," Miss Rachel interrupted, "put the razor carefully on the bookshelf after attempting to wipe it clean—not with her throat spouting like a geyser."

Mr. Krug shut his eyes and looked ill and confused, which was the way Miss Rachel wanted him to look. "No. I see what you mean. I—I put the razor on the bookshelf." His eyes came open with an effect of unutterable woe. "It is my razor, and it was quite a shock, finding it there with Florence's dead body."

Monica cried, "What!"

Miss Jennifer awakened, to stare at all of them owlishly. Miss Rachel felt a twinge of pity; she should have found some way to warn Jennifer not to drink that third cup of tea.

But Mr. Krug seemed unable to keep from answering questions, and he promised some interesting information. Miss Rachel hurried on with: "Can you explain how your razor happened to be there?"

"Not in any manner whatever. I shaved with it yesterday morning, and today I missed it and borrowed an old one of Mr. Carder's."

"Where did you keep it?"

"In the bath which adjoins my room and Mr. Carder's. In the bathroom cabinet. Anyone could have taken it."

"Anyone who knew that you used an old-fashioned straight-edged razor," Miss Rachel answered. "Who *did* know, by the way?"

"Why—everyone, I guess. Except Miss Aldershot, of course. All of the men of the house have seen me shave at one time or another. Even Tommy Hale"—he seemed not to see Monica's jerk of attention—"even Tommy—he was talking to me two days ago in my room. I went in to shave while he was there."

"So that almost anyone might have taken it," Miss Rachel

said half to herself. "And the only value this clue has is that it definitely seems to put the murderer here in the Aldershot house—which we had suspected, anyway," she added silently. To Mr. Krug: "Will you just step in here and write down everything while it's fresh in your mind?"

Mr. Krug dragged himself into Monica's sanctum, begged Monica's pardon for sitting down in it, and began to scribble wearily on a sheet of paper supplied by Miss Rachel.

The room became very quiet—so quiet that the sudden hoarse, constricted breathing of someone in the hall was plainly audible. In an instant Robert Aldershot had come to stand in the door. He was a light ash color, and the skin around his eyes seemed to have been outlined by a knuckle dipped in blue paint. With his gaze on Monica he said, "I've just heard. God, Sis, I can't stand any more! They've got to find out what it's all about. They've got to!" He ran a hand through his hair as though he wanted to pull it out. Inside a heavy purple robe and white silk pajamas his thin frame was shaking.

Monica had sprung up; she went to her brother and put careful and protecting arms around him. "Darling, I didn't want you to know. Not yet. Who told you about Florence?"

"The cook. She didn't realize—— She's not to blame, anyway. I had to know sooner or later." He let Monica lead him in and sit him down beside Mr. Krug, who looked shocked and sympathetic and made clucking sounds meant to be comforting.

"Poor little Florence. Little fool," Robert said bitterly.

"Hush," Monica whispered. "Not here."

"There wasn't anything I couldn't have forgiven. Whatever it was—infidelity, some kid's foolishness—she wasn't more than a kid, even yet——" He broke off to stare around with a tortured manner. "You've got to believe that, all of you. I didn't drive Florence to kill herself. She was my wife. I'd have given her anything in the world she wanted."

"She didn't," Miss Jennifer said suddenly, "kill herself. She was murdered with Mr. Krug's straight-edged razor."

Monica threw a murderous glance over her shoulder, but Robert seemed to have exhausted his emotions and just looked dully at Miss Jennifer. "She's dead," he said finally. "She wouldn't let me help her. There was someone else, some old love. . . . He let her down. I wish I had him here."

Robert Aldershot made a wringing motion with his two hands, and Miss Rachel's vivid imagination put Tommy Hale's neck between them.

She scribbled hastily on her own paper: *Do find out just what Tommy Hale and Florence thought of each other.*

Blushing a little, she added: *Had there been an affair?*

She glanced up to find that Mr. Krug was watching her curiously, and she realized that from where he sat he could see what she had written. It occurred to her that since he knew what was in her mind anyway, she might as well try to pump him on this subject.

"Will you come out into the hall?" she asked. "There's something I'd like to ask you privately."

He stood up and excused himself nervously to Monica. In the hall he let Miss Rachel know with a look that he disapproved of her. "Now, Miss Murdock. Anything you wish, within reason."

"You saw me write this." She let Mr. Krug look at the last two sentences on her paper and pretend to be surprised at them. "Now. You, as general manager here, ought to know, if anyone did, whether Florence and Tommy Hale had indulged in any love-making. The police"—she paused to let the word sink in— "would appreciate any bit of knowledge like this. They might even overlook the trouble you caused them by not reporting Florence's death as soon as you discovered it."

He swallowed and appeared to believe her. "Of course I didn't actually see anything between Tommy and Florence personally. But I believe that some sort of affair had existed at one time. Much before Florence became interested in Mr. Aldershot, and Tommy thought that he—well, before Tommy got some very unfortunate ideas about bettering himself."

"Do you think," Miss Rachel asked, proceeding carefully, "that anyone else knew of this affair?"

"Tim Woodley, poor fellow. He is the one who mentioned it to me. He was laid up with a broken leg, you know—kept him from working afterward—and he had time to do a lot of spying and thinking. Not maliciously. Just to pass the time."

"Did Florence or Tommy know that Tim Woodley had spied on them?"

Mr. Krug floundered in what was obviously deep water. "I couldn't say. Indeed, I couldn't. There was never any open enmity between Tommy and Tim. On the contrary, Tim had taken a sort of fatherly interest in Tommy because the boy was alone."

"And Florence?"

"Tim didn't like her. He made no secret of it. He said that Miss MacConnell was a Scotch—er—witch."

"About your razor," Miss Rachel said, wanting to clear up one point in Mr. Krug's story. "Why did you attempt to clean it and then leave it there with Florence?"

"I scarcely remember what I did. I was shocked to see my razor under such conditions; I had the wild idea that I might be accused——" He caught himself up short. "Understand, I was sure that it was suicide, but there's always the chance of a mistake on the part of the police. I picked up the razor and wiped it on a bit of cloth, silk stuff that was lying on the floor, and then it came to me what I was doing—behaving, really, just as a murderer would. So I put the razor down just anywhere. The bookcase, you said. I left immediately."

"And where was the razor when you first saw it?"

He peered at her. "Why, in Florence's hand. Obviously."

"Which hand?"

"I don't know. Yes, I do. She was lying on her right side with her right hand almost under her body and her left hand flung out. The razor was almost out of sight, half under her body, as though she had dropped it from her right hand in falling."

"That razor," Miss Rachel reminded him, "is going to have your fingerprints on it."

"So it will," he agreed miserably. After a moment of thought he went on: "Will you tell the police that I told you all this in advance, quite freely? It won't be anything like a real check, I know, but it might help. A little."

"I'll tell them." Miss Rachel looked past him, into the little room where Monica's eyes answered hers with a stony stare. "Suppose we join the others now. It might be the tactful thing to do."

"More tactful not to have left them," he muttered miserably, following her back to sit down.

The group was ominously silent in the few minutes that elapsed before the arrival of the police. Robert Aldershot sat in a corner seat; the brown leather upholstery made his skin look sallow and wasted. He had his head slumped backward and his eyes shut. Monica was beside him, one hand tucked between his long slack fingers on the lap of his robe.

Miss Jennifer seemed to have gone back to sleep. Mr. Krug chewed his pencil and breathed harshly through his nose.

Miss Rachel wrote calmly in her neat hand.

We have two murders which are obviously part of the same pattern. I'm going to outline just what I think must have happened, based on the facts as discovered.

Florence MacConnell and Tommy Hale had a love affair which was discovered by Tim Woodley.

The love affair blew over or was broken off, and both Florence and Tommy seemed to have decided to shoot for bigger game. Florence got hers. She married Robert Aldershot, and they went to live in Los Angeles because he expected his family to disapprove of the girl and cause her unhappiness.

Meanwhile, Tommy made progress with Monica but was ridiculed and driven off by Reuben Carder, the uncle. This was the situation when Tim Woodley decided that there was something Robert ought to know and went off to Los Angeles to tell it to him. He had gotten the address from Florence's father in Salinas. The fact that he had disliked Florence, also perhaps that the news he carried concerned her, accounts for the fact that he hid when she came out into the yard of the house in Los Angeles, that he was interested only in the upper bedroom where Robert lay.

Florence and Robert returned to San Cayetano in a mysterious hurry. The story told by both of them was that Robert's condition due to a heart attack was alarming. This was possible, since he was subject to frequent and violent attacks, and the fact of one coming the night before Tim Woodley's murder wasn't too much of a coincidence.

Woodley was run down and carried away in a car belonging to the Aldershots.

Switch then to Florence. She engaged in two telephone conversations—one to Tommy Hale by his own admission—and disappeared. And, incidentally, the song she was singing when she passed Jennifer: "I Can't Give You Anything but Love, Baby." What did it mean?

I'm sure, somehow, that she intended it to mean something.

Florence kept her rendezvous—with death—at about midnight in the tenant house. She was murdered with Mr. Krug's razor, which had been taken from the Aldershot home for the purpose.

Miss Rachel looked up to see Lieutenant Mayhew's huge brown figure in the doorway. He was beckoning her in a very surreptitious manner.

She scribbled hastily before she should forget the thought:

If Florence's past was creeping up on her, why didn't she confess it to an apparently loving and forgiving husband? And would she have used her own indiscretions for the purpose of blackmail?

Miss Rachel stood to go out and then saw the obvious answer. She added hurriedly:

Yes, if it involved Tommy Hale. He was more vulnerable than she; he still had to conquer a strong-willed girl who was far too proud to take Florence MacConnell's cast-off lover.

She went out with the papers clutched in one hand, determined to startle Mayhew with the cleverness of her deductions. All that Mayhew had to do was to check very carefully on Tommy. It was too bad that Tommy was such an overwhelmingly logical suspect; she rather liked the hot-tempered, scornful young man.

Mayhew took her down the corridor a way, out of earshot of the others. He began to talk rapidly in a low voice.

He had taken the map of Woodley's out of his coat pocket and was holding it to the light. Miss Rachel saw again the thin, accurate red lines that outlined the mountain lands, the black scratchings that designated the other Aldershot holdings.

"This," Mayhew said, "was in Woodley's belongings when we

searched them. It's been identified. One of the local officers who is familiar with land operations took this to the county offices and checked it. The red section"—he pointed to the area surrounding the mountain—"is a copy of the map filed in accordance with Federal law by Tommy Hale's father more than thirty years ago, when he homesteaded the lands above the valley."

"You mean—Woodley copied it?"

"Yes. The clerks at the county office remembered him distinctly. He made a request to copy the map in the papers, and so long as the originals aren't harmed, the registry office hasn't any complaint. Woodley copied this drawing more than a month ago. The added section, that drawn in black, doesn't appear on Hale's original map, naturally. It seems to be Woodley's work." Mayhew beat the crackling sheet with a big forefinger. "Whatever the thing is that's behind these killings is up there on that mountain. We're going up at once. Stay here at the Aldershots' until I can see you."

Miss Rachel let her own papers drop to her side, to disappear into the folds of her taffeta skirt.

"I hate going away before I can talk to all of you about Florence MacConnell's—or Aldershot's—death. But this has to be seen to. Now stay put. And stay away from that tenant house as if your life depended upon it. Which it might." He gave her a worried smile, which was meant to be friendly and admonishing at the same time, and walked off through the Aldershot front hallway.

It was really Mayhew's fault, Miss Rachel reflected later, for putting the idea into her head. She had not really thought of going back alone to the tenant house until he mentioned it. She went to the rear door.

San Cayetano was gray bulk against a sky now filled with

clouds. Highlands and meadows swam in the scudding drift; the upper peaks seemed to be smoking chimneys, and the deep clefts were full of darkness. Miss Rachel looked at it from the shelter of the rear porch until she heard the police cars pull away with a roar of motors. Then she went softly toward the pathway through the trees.

Mayhew hadn't been so trusting as to leave the tenant house unguarded. There was a beefy man on the front porch, lounging against the railing with a cigar in his mouth and a watchful eye on the road.

Miss Rachel took care to keep out of his sight. She slid around the back, under the arbor where Reuben Carder liked to catch spiders, and tried the kitchen door silently.

Twilight seemed to have come all with a rush. The light inside the kitchen was just sufficient to make out tables and chairs, the sink, the stove, the dark cavern of the hall. And something else: the sheeted body in the middle of the floor.

CHAPTER XV

THAT WAS as nothing, however, to the further shock that await-
ed her. An instant later Reuben Carder walked in through the
hall door!

He strode in easily and firmly until he saw Miss Rachel. Then
he changed quickly to an invalid's shuffle. "Oh. You here?" He
sounded deliberately rude. "Surprised me. Thought the police
had closed up the place."

Miss Rachel forebore asking him what he was doing in it.
Obviously he had sneaked in in the same manner she had done.
"They haven't taken her away," she said, indicating the body on
its improvised stretcher of planks and bedding.

"They're waiting for the ambulance. Haven't got one in San
Cayetano, you know. Waiting for that creaking old bus out of
Santa Paula. . . . Say, have you seen her?" He flipped the cover
aside in an effort to disgust her.

Miss Rachel looked at the mutilated throat. "I had. Thank
you." She let her eyes rise to his sardonic features. "You don't
have to wonder, do you, where she is now?"

"I?" He laughed; it was loud and merry in the shadowed room.
"You had Mr. Krug doing your work for you, asking her

whereabouts. It occurs to me that Krug must have gone to you this morning as soon as he had found her. Perhaps you instructed him to keep quiet about it."

He was adjusting the sheet across the still, upturned face. "What makes you think Krug was doing my job?"

"I think that you had plans for Florence. She might be useful to keep Tommy Hale away from Monica."

"What strange ideas you have," he complained. "I'm a hired man just as Krug is. I wouldn't dare dictate to Monica. She'd laugh at me."

"She hasn't so far."

"And Tommy," he continued, "why, I almost like the kid. He's a rude young brute, too big for his britches, insulting whenever he feels in the mood for it." He rose, made a deprecating gesture with a long hand. "As for his affair with Florence"—he coughed a little—"haven't we all been foolish at one time or another?"

The body between them made a white blotch in the gloom, and Miss Rachel thought suddenly of the dead brain there, the brain that had been alive and full of scheming; the brain that must have protested Carder's easy scorn had it heard.

The silence spun out, and the room was perceptibly darker.

"Do you know," Carder said on a quiet note, "that if I were you I should move out of this house?"

A drop of ice water seemed to start at the edge of Miss Rachel's hair and slide to a spot between her shoulder blades, where it penetrated to her heart. But she didn't quit looking at the dark face under its cap of snow-white hair. "We can't leave just yet. My sister needs the dry air and the altitude."

"Noses are used for other things than breathing. But breathing's much healthier." He made for the door in his sly pretense at shuffling; his eyes mocked as he went past, laughing at himself for his acting. "I'd keep my sister on the right track. And the dry air won't do you any harm either, Miss Murdock."

She looked after him as his figure vanished into the outer gloom. "If your business needs poking into, I'll poke my nose into it," she said angrily, but under her breath. "And the dry air wouldn't hurt *you*, Mr. Carder. Suppose you concentrate on it for once."

She went immediately upstairs, still rather cross, and got a handkerchief from her room; the handkerchief was to be her excuse for coming, in case the police found her. Then, back in the hall, she stood still and listened. The detective on the front porch was walking now, warming himself by plodding up and down the narrow space. "I'll take just a brief look in the attic," she promised guiltily. She went back to her room for the flashlight, turned its glow into the boxlike stairway to the attic. On the lower treads was a scattering of torn paper like a thin fall of snow.

Miss Rachel gathered it bit by bit and then went up. But though she prowled the scene of the crime for many minutes, got much dust on herself, and left the place noticeably more ordered, she had little for her pains. All evidence had been removed, and, to Lieutenant Mayhew's careful mind, practically everything was evidence. Florence's suitcase, the spilled purse and its contents, the remains of lunch and of cigarettes were gone. There was the bare floor with its dreadful stain; nothing more.

She went back by way of the kitchen and the grove path to the Aldershot house. Monica and Uncle Reuben and Robert were in Monica's little sanctum, talking in low tones. Miss Jennifer, Mr. Krug, and Jeff Woodley were seated at a little table in the pantry. The housekeeper was serving them coffee in what were obviously the kitchen cups.

When Miss Rachel walked in Jeff Woodley was just finishing what he was saying: "—and so they said to come back home; there wasn't anythin' more I could help them with. They went through Tim's stuff the way folks do in these here spy pictures. Didn't find a darned thing. I tried to tell them Tim wasn't the writin' kind; he carried what he knew in his head, but they wouldn't believe me. They said he'd had a map, didn't he?"

Miss Rachel slid into the extra chair and answered Jeff's sad nod of greeting with a smile.

"I told them I didn't see any point in the map; it was Aldershot lands, and maybe Tim made it just for somethin' to do." He drew in a sip of coffee with a long inhaling sound. "Maybe Tim thought there was somethin' wrong with the Aldershot titles. If he did he was crazy. Old man Aldershot bought stuff for keeps."

Miss Rachel took out the torn bits of paper and began arranging them on the oilcloth-covered surface of the table. Slowly, piece by piece, a design began to emerge. It was a rough duplicate of the map about which Jeff Woodley had been speaking.

He was watching with his sad eyes widened. "Say, that looks sort of familiar."

"It should look familiar, Mr. Woodley. It's a copy of your brother's map. Not a good copy, I'm afraid."

There was a peculiar aberration in the map. To the right of San Cayetano the outline of the mountain lands had been changed. The former border between the early Aldershot holdings and those bought from Tommy Hale's father had been scratched out crudely with pencil, a new line drawn that brought the slate pit, represented by a black dot, into the section representing the valley lands.

Jeff Woodley noticed the difference immediately. "'Tain't

exactly right there. The old slate pit was on Hale's land. Never belonged to the Aldershot properties until old man Aldershot bought it off him."

Miss Rachel was staring at the map, but she was not speaking her thoughts. Obviously this discovery put an entirely new light on everything. Finding the paper on the attic stairs would seem to indicate that it was connected with Florence's vigil there. Had Florence had it? If so, it would mean that she knew what the map represented, and the emphasis must shift from the details of her involved love life into other matters entirely.

But if Florence had carried it there, who had found it afterward and torn it up? And why leave the scraps on the stairs, where they were easily found?

She felt that she was on the verge of a reasonable answer to this last question when Lieutenant Mayhew walked in at the door.

He spoke to all of them, listened without comment while Miss Rachel explained her new clue. He looked at the reconstructed copy with a frown between his heavy brows, sat down slowly to study it in detail. He, too, saw the change in outline almost at once.

"It's absolutely wrong here." He touched the wavering line that curved away to include the slate pit. "Before dark closed in we reached the pit, and from it we located the old boundary. There are still a few of Hale's original stakes left in the ground. The boundary passes far below the slate pit. I wonder who drew this, and why?"

"Someone who had had a look at Woodley's map, obviously," Miss Rachel said, "but who didn't have it at hand to copy. The whole outline is bigger and less in proportion than his, and there are smaller inaccuracies—differences, rather. For instance, the

Aldershot home is shown as it actually is, on a branch driveway, and not as Woodley had it, directly on the road."

"So I see." Mayhew's voice was grim, tired too. "That little detail might give us something. Who would trouble to correct such a mistake in Woodley's map except someone who lives on the property and knows it too well to let the error pass? I think we may assume that the map was drawn by one of the household here."

Mr. Krug, who had not said anything, drew a long gasping breath.

"Finding it where I did is a puzzler," Miss Rachel said, capturing the thought that Mayhew's entrance had interrupted, "but one possibility may be that the map was found by someone who didn't know its meaning, who tore it up carelessly as nothing of value, and let the scraps fall where they may. Incidentally, I ran into Mr. Carder in the tenant house when I went there for my handkerchief."

Lieutenant Mayhew made a wry mouth at the word "handkerchief," but he also lost no time in taking Miss Rachel with him to find Monica's uncle. He left instructions that the others were to leave the map as it was for further examination later. In the hall he paused. "Let me handle Carder my way," he said. "If you go at him he'll get his back up."

"I wonder," she meditated, "just why he dislikes me so?"

"You've been poaching on his territory." Mayhew let a smile break through the grimness for an instant. "Up until now Uncle Reuben has fancied himself as the family spy. Having himself bundled up in a wheel chair was a wonderful idea for his purposes. Kept him safely away from strenuous labor too."

Miss Rachel was astonished. "How did you know? I knew

this afternoon because he walked into the kitchen as well as any-one could. But you didn't see him."

"I didn't have to. Carder's legs are well muscled; the flesh on them is firm. I could see that, and I knew that he wasn't actually the invalid he pretends to be. If he were, his legs would be shriv-eled and flabby."

Miss Rachel nibbled her lower lip thoughtfully. Really, she considered, Mayhew was getting very shrewd. The thought worried her a little. She wanted him to feel that he needed her. She should have noticed Carder's legs and pointed them out to Mayhew.

Curiosity, however, was prodding her on another point. "What about your trip up San Cayetano? Did you find anything?"

"We found a barrier in the road which must have been put there to keep the public out of the Aldershot holdings up there. We found the pit—it's a ghastly thing. Sides straight down, slate like a polished toboggan slide. Don't go near it."

"You took the barrier down?"

Mayhew nodded. "We're going to keep an eye out to see who tries to rebuild it. Not that I have much hope anyone will try. Whoever knows the secret of that mountain must know that we're working closer to it every hour and that the safest thing is to stay away."

They had reached the door of Monica's little sanctum. Reuben Carder was alone there, sitting in his wheel chair with his face turned toward the windows and his back to the lighted room. He swung the wheel chair slowly at the sound of Mayhew's step.

"Just a few questions, Mr. Carder."

Reuben Carder's eyes went past the detective to settle on Miss Rachel. His mouth twisted under the white mustache. "Certainly. About my trip to the tenant house, obviously, since you have Miss Murdock with you, and I've come to suspect by now that she's the stooge of the police. Begin, Lieutenant. The why, the when, and the where."

"Since you've suggested it," Mayhew said, composed, "suppose you begin with the why of your visit."

"Curiosity. I've never seen the victim of a brutal crime before. Such sights belong in everyone's education. My nephew Harley accompanied me, incidentally, but he's a bit young for such advanced studies. He was out in the grove, being sick, I think, when Miss Murdock met me."

"How long were you in the house?"

"Not long. Not over ten or fifteen minutes."

"And the where," Mayhew concluded. "Did you get as far as the attic?"

He started to answer and then checked himself and looked both at Miss Rachel and at Mayhew carefully. "I think you know, somehow, that I did. So I'll admit it. Yes, I went up there where she was killed."

"And you did what?"

"Looked for evidence, as any amateur sleuth does. Tucked into the wall timbers I found a scrap of paper which I at first took to be a clue and then discarded as worthless."

"And what sort of paper was this?"

Carder waved a negligent hand. "A botch of a map. Some child's play, a scribbled thing."

"Would it surprise you to know that we think Tim Woodley died because of what was contained on a duplicate of that paper?"

Carder became very still. His ears took on the listening look that Miss Rachel had noted before. His green eyes swung back to the windows. "Indeed? I can't think so; I can't agree to it."

"Why not?"

"There wasn't anything indicated on the paper I saw which isn't common knowledge in this whole valley. And it wasn't accurate."

"Woodley's original map was quite accurate so far as the mountain lands formerly owned by Hale were concerned. There had been changes made in this crude copy, of course."

"The slate pit," Carder agreed. "Still, it can't mean anything. If mining had been done, if evidence had been found of some mineral deposits—— But there has been nothing like that. Nothing at all."

Mayhew's whole face had settled into an angry stillness. "And just why should the finding of mineral deposits make any difference?"

Carder gave his bombshell proper timing. He waited a moment or two, seemed to study the darkening view outside the windows, where San Cayetano stood black against the masses of boiling clouds and where the last traces of gray light shone from the west like the gleam from a candle into an abyss.

"The mineral rights aren't always sold with the land in this part of the country. I don't know what the laws are in other states. In California the law gives the owner of mineral rights the privilege of tearing up the ground to get at anything under it—no matter who owns the surface and agricultural rights. There have been instances of bitter feelings. . . . However, there are no groves to be damaged on the heights of San Cayetano. And no gold under the earth there, either."

Mayhew's mind was quick. "But Hale had reserved these rights?"

"I believe so." Carder's eyes were perfectly inscrutable. "There is usually a time limit set on these things. You might see how long Hale's rights have yet to run."

Mayhew didn't wait for further suggestions. He went out into the hall and was heard shortly at the telephone, demanding to be put in touch with the county offices.

"They'll be closed, of course," Carder said to Miss Rachel. "Oh, Harley, there you are. Come in, boy. You've met Miss Murdock?"

Miss Rachel nodded at the boy who looked so much like Monica. He walked into the room with the easy slouch of youth. "Uncle Reuben, you're missing something. You ought to go and take a look at Monica."

"Where is Monica?" Carder asked without too much interest.

"On the back porch." Harley grinned at some secret and walked about the room, flipping the pages of magazines and books. "You wouldn't like what she's doing. Uh-*uh*."

Carder was nettled. "Well, what is she doing?"

"She's kissing Tommy Hale in what they fondly imagine is pitch-darkness. Two detectives are watching them from the driveway, and this lady's sister"—he nodded toward Miss Rachel—"is about to break her neck staring at them from the pantry window."

CHAPTER XVI

MISS RACHEL went away discreetly to look for her sister. But she had noted that Reuben Carder didn't seem discomposed at the knowledge of Monica's behavior with Tommy Hale. Either Carder had told the truth in saying that he didn't care whether or not his niece loved young Hale, or he was playing a part for Miss Rachel's benefit.

"I'll file you away," Miss Rachel said mentally to the man in the wheel chair, "and study you in detail later."

She found Lieutenant Mayhew at the telephone, demanding that the county offices be opened and the records checked on the Hale properties. As Miss Rachel went past Mayhew glared at her, evidently associating her with the reluctant fool on the other end of the line, and then, realizing who she was, he forced himself to smile.

She found Miss Jennifer in the pantry. Jeff Woodley and Mr. Krug had gone. The housekeeper was clearing away the supper things, and Miss Jennifer was disgracefully peeping under the blind.

"What's happening now?" Miss Rachel asked coolly.

"He's holding her hands and saying something. She's trying

to put her fingers on his mouth. From what I can hear, it seems he's accusing himself of all sorts of things. Rudeness and self-ishness and stupidity——" Her voice came to a halt. It must have occurred to Miss Jennifer that the last question hadn't been asked by the housekeeper.

"Young people quarrel and make up without much reason," Miss Rachel commented. "Don't you think so, Jennifer?"

Miss Jennifer came away from the blind full of embarrass-ment. "I suppose that they do," she said meekly. Then, remem-bering Miss Rachel's departure with Mayhew, "What did you find out from Mr. Carder?"

"He found the map, as I rather thought he had, and discard-ed it as worthless. The map was tucked into some beams in the attic." Miss Rachel, seeing that the housekeeper was out of ear-shot in the kitchen, clutched Miss Jennifer's fingers in her own. "We've got to leave, Jennifer. We must get back to the tenant house and spend the night there. We'll have to leave here before Lieutenant Mayhew tells us we mustn't."

"But why?" Miss Jennifer cried in horror.

"Reasons." Miss Rachel pulled her into the hall and by way of a side door out upon the driveway. The air was cold, and big drops of rain spattered them now and then from a sky bulging with black clouds.

From some place of vigil Samantha had joined them. Her lonesome howls threatened to betray them to the others in-side the house until Miss Rachel picked her up and carried her. Where the pathway ended on the clearing at the tenant house they paused. A big ambulance stood by the kitchen door, and white-coated men were removing Florence MacConnell's body.

"Rachel, we're—we're crazy," Miss Jennifer moaned. "To sleep in a house with a dead body just gone out of it, with that woman's blood over our heads, with heaven only knows what sort of fiend just waiting to get at us."

"It's the telephone I'm after," Miss Rachel explained. "I noticed one in the tenant house, and though I haven't had occasion to use it—Monica called the police on the one at her home—I'm pretty sure that it's kept in working order. Most of the time the place was occupied by employees, and the telephone would be convenient to get hold of them."

The big ambulance was swinging away from the house; its head lamps showed the rain falling in an irregular pattern through the dark.

"When we use the telephone we can leave again?" Miss Jennifer asked hopefully.

"No."

They waited while the ambulance sped out toward the road with its tires hissing on the gravel, and a further while to give the detective Mayhew had left on guard time to make up his mind about leaving. He ambled toward them finally, his big feet making a crunching sound and his voice complaining quietly at the rain. They drew in among the trees to let him pass.

"There goes civilization," Miss Jennifer whimpered. "Now we might as well be in the African jungle among head-hunters."

"Borneo," Miss Rachel corrected. "Let's make a run for the kitchen. He's probably locked it, but I have a key in my pocket." At the door she put the cat down to search. When she had found the key and unlocked the door and pushed it open, she warned, "Not a sound, Jennifer. And no lights for a minute, either."

They stood in the dark room and listened. From above came the rattle of rain on shingles and the creak of the old house as moisture soaked into it, but no sound of footfall or of other movement.

Miss Rachel snapped on the lights, and Miss Jennifer took in a long breath of relief.

The telephone in the hallway proved to be in working order. Miss Rachel asked the village operator for the number of the boy who delivered groceries for the store. Connected with Johnny's home, she heard the comforting sound of his young masculine voice in her ear.

When she was sure that Johnny remembered who she was she broached the subject of her call. "I have to make an early trip tomorrow and I was wondering if you could take the truck to drive me. I'll be leaving much earlier than the store will need you, and the trip won't be a long one."

"I'd like to oblige you," Johnny said agreeably. "Where was it you needed to go?"

"I'll explain that in the morning."

"Well, it isn't my truck, you know. Belongs to Mr. Bowron. I don't think he'd mind, if you're willing to buy what gas we'd use."

"And I'd insist on paying you for your trouble, Johnny. Shall we say at five?"

"Five in the morning?" said Johnny uncertainly.

"I know it's asking a lot."

"Not a bit. I'll be seeing you."

Miss Rachel thanked him and hung up.

"Where on earth," Miss Jennifer cried, "can you be going at five o'clock tomorrow morning?"

"We're going up San Cayetano."

"But why? Didn't Lieutenant Mayhew just come back from there?"

"He didn't find anything because it got dark too soon and, besides, he didn't know then what he was looking for."

"And what was he looking for?"

"Some sign of mining activity. Excavations, tunnels, things like that." She explained briefly what Carder had told them about Hale's reservation of mineral rights. "You see, that must be the bedrock of the whole thing, Hale's mineral rights. I suppose he left them to Tommy. That means, according to law, as Mr. Carder explained it, that Tommy can go up there on land that supposedly belongs to the Aldershots and take out whatever is worth taking if it comes under the head of minerals."

"Gold?" Miss Jennifer wondered, her thin face full of thought. "I suppose there must be a great deal of undiscovered gold in California. It couldn't all have been found in '49."

"We'll concentrate on the slate pit," Miss Rachel said. "If you remember the map I found on the attic steps, you recall that it was drawn in such a way that the slate pit was included with the original Aldershot valley lands. I have the most peculiar hunch about that map, Jennifer. It looks to me as though that changed boundary line represented wishful thinking on someone's part."

"Florence's?"

"I wonder. As an Aldershot, she would be enriched by any increase in their total wealth."

They were interrupted by the sound of knocking at the kitchen door.

Mayhew put a brown stern face in at them. "What on earth," he wondered, "made you come back here?"

"Bed," Miss Rachel said briefly.

He studied her as though the memory of the old tricks she had played on him was a nettle in his thoughts. "I don't believe I'd sleep here if I were you. Miss Aldershot can put you up." He waited for a reaction and got none. "Or I could call a police car. You might like to go back to Los Angeles."

Miss Rachel's eyes grew bright. "Really, Lieutenant."

He had the decency to blush. "I was thinking of your safety entirely. I don't want to steal your thunder."

"Perhaps," she suggested forgivingly, "you could sleep here. We'd feel safe then. There's a bed upstairs that Jennifer refuses to sleep in. I'm sure you'd be comfortable."

It was settled that way finally. Mayhew joined them in a cup of tea, and they went upstairs afterward to the sound of rain on the roof and the groan of a rising wind.

"Good night," Mayhew said. He turned in his doorway and looked thoughtfully at Miss Rachel's lock. There was, Miss Rachel noted gratefully, no key in it. Otherwise, she thought, Mayhew might have tried some juvenile trick of fastening them in.

Miss Jennifer shivered. "Cold, beastly place."

Miss Rachel's mind had turned to other matters. "What about Hale's mineral rights? Did you rouse the county offices?"

"I roused them," Mayhew said grimly. "They won't be so sassy for a long time again." The memory of his work on the telephone made his mouth twitch. "Hale's mineral rights were reserved, just as Carder suggested they were. They've got a little less than a year to go. See what you make of that, along with the rest of the mess, and tell me about it in the morning."

The doors shut between them. Miss Rachel walked to the bed and sat down on the edge of it. Miss Jennifer started to disrobe, then stopped to watch curiously.

"What is it, Rachel?"

Miss Rachel's eyes were big and dark in her small face. "I'm afraid, Jennifer. Not for us. Not for myself. For someone else. You see, poor Tim Woodley and Florence MacConnell were killed because they *knew*. They knew of some shenanigans in connection with those mineral rights—shenanigans either on the part of the one who owns them or of someone who wants them. . . ."

In either connection someone else will obviously have to know soon. There will be some sort of legal palaver when the mineral rights run out; there has to be. And then——"

Miss Jennifer finished undressing in a hurry. "These Aldershots—don't you think they're an unwholesome lot, Rachel? I mean introverted and unsound, or whatever a psychologist would call them. Mentally molded, sort of."

"They've lived too long in the shade. San Cayetano puts its shadow over them, and, as you say, they've molded."

Miss Jennifer crept under the bedclothes as Rachel rose to undress. "And you think someone else is in danger?"

"I'm sure of it. We'll have to hurry. I hope we can get away in the morning without Lieutenant Mayhew knowing."

The early light showed the continuing drizzle, the wet, glittering green trees, the brown earth turned in rows like soaked corduroy. Miss Rachel slid out of bed into chilly grayness and peeped through the window. San Cayetano seemed to waver in the watery sky, the shoulder of a giant who crouched with his head down to weep.

"Wake up, Jennifer. Don't make any sound."

They stole presently down through the dark hall and the stairs, paused for a hurried cup of tea, then went out upon the front porch to wait for Johnny. He swung in from the highway, tires spattering the puddles in the drive. Just as they drove off Miss Rachel thought she heard some sort of movement in the house—Mayhew pounding downstairs, perhaps. She looked carefully in the opposite direction. If Mayhew came out to try to flag them down she didn't want to see him.

The road up San Cayetano's flank was slippery and treacherous, and Johnny drove with his nose close to the windshield and his eyes big with worry. He didn't try to sing or to talk about his girl friend. His single comment was, "Cold, isn't it?" which seemed the signal for Miss Jennifer to shiver.

They reached unfamiliar ground at last; the road leveled toward a long meadow near whose edge a crater gaped.

Looking down into the slate pit a few minutes later, Miss Rachel felt disappointment sweep over her. It wasn't the bottomless chasm of her imaginings, black as night with a suggestion of slime in its lower reaches. It was simply a pit from which slate had been mined, leaving smooth, unbroken surfaces which would, no doubt, keep anything imprisoned permanently, man or beast, which fell into it.

Miss Rachel explained to Johnny what they had come to look for. "Signs of mining. Fresh earth. Anything covered with loose brush. A hole which seems to have been dug recently."

"I get it," Johnny commented. "You think somebody's been prospecting and you want to find out where." He scouted away, rubbing the thin rain off his face.

Miss Rachel walked the length of the meadow and returned. There were, so far as she could see, no signs of digging or of searching. She looked for footprints under the wet brush, found some which she decided had been made by the men with Mayhew yesterday. At last she went to the edge of the meadow, pushed through brush, and looked off across the valley. Clouds ran like smoke before the wind, and the rain had washed out colors and made everything gray. Nevertheless, it was all there in a panorama to take away the breath. The village, toy houses on a toy street; the hills beyond with their oil derricks thin and black and fine. Little gray hills, Miss Rachel thought, their earth having a touch of blue in it. Wasn't it the color, too, of San Cayetano?

The space, the sense of highness and remoteness chilled her, and she turned back.

Miss Jennifer was at the edge of the slate pit, teetering on her toes, looking in. A cry rose in Miss Rachel's throat; choked off as Miss Jennifer's skirts whipped at her ankles in a sudden gust. Miss Jennifer took an uneasy step backward, lost her balance, poised there with her arms flapping.

Miss Rachel began to run. Out of the corners of her eyes she saw Johnny, good boy, running too. Miss Jennifer let out a high scream and began to slide in over the lip of the slate pit.

That sense of slowness which possesses one in nightmares came over Miss Rachel. Her legs were wooden and clumsy; clumps of brush and big stones got in her way; there was the feeling of swimming upstream against a heavy current. And all the while there was Jennifer's falling body, struggling to keep from slipping over, and yet slipping over anyway. Jennifer's face, white with agony and fear, looked back at her, and one of Jennifer's hands clutched at a bit of grass. A pitiful bit, withered and shrunken and bowed down by the rain.

It was that bit of grass, however, that saved her. Unexpectedly firm, it resisted her pulling. The roots went deep, and the rain had made them tough. The earth began to give, but by then Miss Rachel and Johnny had reached her. Miss Jennifer promptly fainted.

She looked little and woebegone lying in the wet grass with a frosting of rain on her. Miss Rachel bent over her, murmuring passionate and condemnatory reproaches for herself. If she hadn't insisted on coming to San Cayetano this wouldn't have happened. If she had listened to Jennifer they would by now be safe at home in Los Angeles instead of on the side of a gloomy mountain, beaten with rain and frozen with the wind. She rubbed Jennifer's wrists, took off her own jacket to wrap about Jennifer's legs.

She saw it then—the black ooze on Jennifer's slippers. All of the reproach and the regret went out of Miss Rachel instantly. She shook Johnny in a fever of excitement.

Johnny put a finger to the black ooze and smelled it cautiously. "You're right," he granted. "In the pit, too, wasn't it?"

They peered in over the edge, neglecting to notice that Jennifer had revived and joined them.

"Oil," Miss Rachel whispered. "It was oil, all the time!"

CHAPTER XVII

A SECTION of slate had fallen away, and a black surface was exposed; a glassy surface which tainted the air with the musky smell of oil.

"It's been covered up," Johnny said. "That slab of rock was loose. It had been propped there."

Miss Rachel's gaze was thoughtful. "I wonder just how long ago this seepage of oil was found. Not at the time Tommy Hale's father died here—something would have been done about it by now."

"Providing," Miss Jennifer pointed out in a weak voice, "that Tommy knew about it. Suppose one of the Aldershots had found the oil? Would they have told Tommy about it when chances were the passing of time would give the oil to them? Not likely."

"Even old man Aldershot——" Johnny touched the sticky surface cautiously. "Suppose he knew? Suppose he coached the rest of them about covering up until Tommy's mineral rights ran out?"

"Since we're supposing," Miss Rachel said, "let's try to figure what Tommy would have done if he had known. Would he have run about broadcasting his news? He doesn't impress me as the type. I think he'd keep very quiet about the oil until he found some money, some backing to take care of the development. And then—if by the time he'd found the backers willing to drill his wells for him his precious mineral rights were almost gone— what then? After the way the Aldershots had treated him, it's my guess he'd go to almost any lengths to keep them from knowing what they were getting."

"Perhaps trying to marry Monica was an attempt to safeguard himself in case he couldn't find the capital to drill," Miss Jennifer put in.

"Gee," Johnny exclaimed, "you make it sound as though any of them might be guilty!"

Miss Rachel arose and brushed the wet grass from her skirt. "Any of them might," she said softly. "Don't look now, but there's the lieutenant looking at us from the other side of the meadow, and I've a hunch he's rather angry."

Mayhew lumbered toward them like a brown bear. His eyes were like two pieces of flint, and his mouth was ready for bitter words. Miss Rachel forestalled him.

"I suppose you knew about this. You might have told us and saved us a trip up here." She indicated the bleeding ooze where the slate had been.

Mayhew knew that she was trying to soothe him by making him defend himself before he could start what he had meant to say. He swung on his big heels and gave a glance into the pit. "Thanks for finding it," he snapped. "We thought that's what must be here. The whole valley's gone oil-mad since those wells were put in on the other ridge a year ago and proved to be good producers. There is a geological fault which continues through San Cayetano into the back country. People have been expecting oil to be found up here for a long time."

"But just who," Johnny wondered, "knew this was in the pit?"

"I think we can name two who knew it," Mayhew answered grimly. "Tim Woodley and Florence MacConnell Aldershot. They died for knowing. If it weren't for the fact that two scraps of paper showed up bearing maps of the mountain, we might never have known why they died. Woodley—unintentionally, I think—left his map among his belongings when he went off to try to find Robert Aldershot in Los Angeles. The girl must have had sense enough to hide her copy in the attic rafters when she guessed what might be in store for her. The murderer obviously wouldn't have left it there."

"You're clearing Mr. Carder of any suspicion, then," Miss Rachel pointed out. "He wouldn't have torn the map and left the scraps on the stairs if he wished to conceal what the paper was."

"Mr. Carder's account of how the scraps of paper came to be on the stairs can't be verified," Mayhew warned. "Suppose someone else had found and scattered the paper before the murderer could retrieve it? Wouldn't it be, then, the murderer's place to say he'd done it, since the act indicated ignorance of the map's meaning?"

When Mayhew had stopped speaking the high whine of a car's motor could be heard on the grade below. A few moments later Monica's coupé burst through the driving mist to stop beside Mayhew's at the other end of the meadow. Monica alighted, slim and erect inside blue slacks and a yellow sweater. She walked around the car and opened the door for Robert. Robert got out and hugged his overcoat to him and looked at the group by the pit with cavernous eyes.

"What goes on? What are you all doing here on my property?"

Mayhew is singularly impatient with people who own property which the law needs for its own uses. "Official business," he snapped. "This concerns the murder of your wife and of Woodley."

"The pit?" Robert said blankly.

Monica had her arm through his. "We've been very patient, Lieutenant. We've allowed you free rein in your investigations. We even—at my brother's insistence—co-operated in the silly game these two little old ladies were playing, pretending to have come here for their health. Robert recognized them———"

Robert's hand had jerked her arm. "Let me explain, Monica. Yes, Miss Murdock, I did recognize you. You were my neighbor in Los Angeles. When Monica came back and told me of Woodley's murder———"

Miss Rachel interrupted in her turn. "But you didn't *know* of Woodley's murder! Not then! Not that night you told Monica to play up to us!"

A steely glaze came into his eyes, and his thin face darkened. "Monica had been in the village. Krug had made some mention of seeing Florence at Mrs. Simpson's place, and Monica slipped in there to see her. She didn't know then that Florence and I were married, but she suspected that something was wrong somewhere. While she was in the hall at Mrs. Simpson's, wondering which room she should look for Florence in, she heard the radio broadcast of the discovery of Woodley's body. The news meant nothing to her until she heard that a couple who had lived at a certain address was being hunted in connection with the crime. The address she recognized—it had been the one I had given her as my own."

"Neat," Miss Rachel said soundlessly to herself. "Very neat. Tidy, with no loose ends. But why was Monica, Krug, and company trying to find Florence? Were they all in on it? Is it a case of a mass of murderers, a conspiracy?"

It was as though Monica could read her thoughts. The sulky eyes fixed on the little old lady in taffeta. "Florence had changed Robert so dreadfully, you see. All of his worry, his nervousness began with his interest in her. I had to know, to find out somehow what she meant to him, what right she had to make a mess of his life with her cheap, vixenish pranks. If there was something deeper than flirtation, as Robert thought there was; if Florence was part of a plot to entice Robert away——"

"Why," Miss Rachel wondered aloud, "should Florence have enticed Robert away from something which wasn't his?"

Monica looked blank. "I don't understand."

Miss Rachel pointed delicately down into the pit. "There is an oil seepage there which would seem to indicate that a great deal of this smelly but valuable stuff lies under the earth. It's your earth, Monica. Yours and your brothers'. But the oil belongs to Tommy—at least until his rights to it run out."

The thing that happened to Monica then was so unexpected, so quiet, and yet so dramatic, that it left all of them standing like fools in a stupor of utter silence. Monica looked suddenly like a child—a bewildered, lost child who has a light flashed in its face and finds itself in the midst of a terrifying strangeness. She became quite pale. And then she folded inside the slacks; the pale hair slid over her face, and she was a soundless bundle at her brother's feet.

Robert looked at them wildly. "What does it mean? What's it all about? Oil? You've frightened Monica terribly." He bent over her, and the pale hair fell away to reveal a face like paper.

"Perhaps she has guessed," Miss Jennifer whispered into her sister's ear, "that Tommy has been playing up to her for his own purposes. It would be a shock, wouldn't it?"

But Miss Rachel was studying Monica's uplifted face. The fine rain had begun to frost the platinum hair, and under the lashes something glittered: a raindrop or a tear. Miss Rachel went and knelt beside Monica and put an arm under her shoulders.

"Steady," she murmured. "Don't overdo it, and the lieutenant won't ever guess."

Monica's eyes flew open. She looked stung with shame. "I'm quite all right. I'll be myself in a minute."

"Don't you think that Tommy has really loved you?" said Miss Rachel, almost inaudibly.

The stung look intensified, became bitter, secretive.

"That isn't very important now, is it?"

"It may be," Miss Rachel answered. "Do you love him?"

Monica pulled away. Her whisper was almost without sound. "I do."

"Would you still love him if you knew he'd done these crimes?"

"Yes; I'm a bitch, I suppose, but I would." She began to brush particles of soil off her sweater and allowed the lieutenant and Robert to help her rise.

The group stood for a moment in the rain; there was a feeling of letdown, of anticlimax. Neither Robert nor Monica showed any interest in the oil seepage. Mayhew indicated the parked cars with a nod. "We might as well go. I'll see you at the house."

Monica stumbled away, and Robert followed more slowly. Mayhew told Johnny to run along; he'd see that the Misses Murdock got safely back. Johnny, whose taste for detective work had only just been whetted, went lingeringly.

"I thought you'd question Monica a bit," Miss Rachel said innocently.

"I intend to. First I thought I'd find out just what you and she were whispering about." All patience had vanished from Mayhew's voice. "It's just at times like these that you do get a bit infuriating. Coaching a girl who's practically given the show away: that's bad."

Miss Rachel shook her head. "You're quite wrong, Lieutenant, but I forgive you." She didn't stop to hear what Mayhew had to say to this; he looked ready to explode, and she hurried on. "Monica hadn't given any show away. She was putting on one. A very creditable performance too. Except that people don't shed tears while they're unconscious. All I did was to surprise her by letting her know that I, at least, hadn't been taken in."

"And what precious item," Mayhew said grimly, "did she let drop?"

"Really, *Mr. Mayhew.*"

This utterly formal address brought Mayhew up short and reminded him of Miss Rachel's hold over him. Miss Rachel had had the good fortune to have saved from murder the girl whom Mayhew had since married.* She had, in Mayhew's opinion, taken full advantage of this fact, but he had no desire to face his wife were she to know that he had been anything but patient and courteous to Miss Rachel. So he flushed and endured.

Miss Rachel, seeing Mayhew put back into his proper place, continued: "She gave out that she really loves Tommy Hale. That's very important. I believe you'd better put a tail on Tommy."

This bit of professional verbiage made Mayhew blink.

"If Tommy is guilty he'll try to get away. If he isn't guilty I believe someone will try to kill him. Either way, he can do with one of your detectives."

"Why kill him," Mayhew argued, "when his mineral rights will soon run out anyway?"

"They wouldn't run out soon enough. A well could be put

* *The Cat Saw Murder*

down and enough oil taken out—providing the well was as good as you say the others are—to make Tommy quite independently wealthy, even in the time he has left. Our murderer would hate that."

"Providing it isn't Tommy himself."

"Providing." Miss Rachel and Mayhew had begun to walk toward Mayhew's car. Miss Jennifer remained for a last cautious peep into the slate pit.

"And why do you think Monica's loving this kid is so important?" Mayhew asked, reverting to Miss Rachel's original statement.

"Because so much has been done to make sure that she didn't," Miss Rachel answered. "Her uncle seems to have worked hard at breaking the affair up. Robert offered a sort of passive resistance, to judge from his attitude the night I spied on him and Monica. The younger brother teased and made fun." She paused to watch Monica's coupé as it swung off through the rain. "The fact that she's gone on loving him anyway marks her as a sort of outsider to her family. She doesn't see eye to eye with them. I think that's very important."

Miss Jennifer joined them, and they drove through mist and fine rain and found the road like a yellow slash on the smooth flank of the mountain. Johnny's truck was ahead, throwing a muddy wake; far below, Monica's coupé slid dangerously, skidding at the lip of the valley.

"She's driving too fast," Miss Rachel said worriedly.

"Honk at her or something," suggested Miss Jennifer.

"There's nothing I can do." Mayhew rubbed a mist off the windshield and stared at the car below with narrowed eyes. Johnny's horn bleated warningly, but the coupé raced on. At the turn below the wheels spun and the car lurched sidewise, struck the embankment, and then roared away with a new burst of speed. A broken fender flapped in the wind. Miss Rachel thought she heard the screech of metal as it tore away completely and rolled at the side of the road.

Miss Rachel put her hands together in her lap. "Hurry!" she whispered.

Mayhew bit at his lower lip. "Can't do much on this road. It's——" He grasped the wheel and turned it sharply; for an instant the sheer drop yawned before the front wheels and then vanished. Mayhew began to perspire. "It's too dangerous to hurry."

"Even for you," Miss Rachel added unconsciously, remembering Mayhew's frenzied methods in town. "She must be past seeing the road. What's happened to her?"

But when they reached the courtyard behind the Aldershot house Monica's coupé sat there ordinarily enough. Robert stood by it; there was a blank, cold expression in his eyes as he watched them drive up.

Mayhew jumped out and pounded toward him. "Where's your sister?"

He motioned briefly toward the house. "Inside. She's—upset. Something about young Hale. I didn't understand." He looked tired, sick, but he made no move to follow Mayhew as the detective ran for the back entry.

Miss Rachel hurried, holding her skirts so they wouldn't trip her, angry at the mass of petticoats that Jennifer thought was proper. The hall was gloomy; Mayhew's form up ahead was a black bulk against the open door of Monica's little study.

Mayhew sprang into the room with an angry cry, and there

was a sharp scream in a woman's voice and the loud report of a gun.

Miss Rachel almost fell over herself getting to the door. There was Mayhew—Monica also. A gun lay on the floor between them.

They were utterly still and without movement, and the quiet in the little room was to Miss Rachel like the very presence of death itself.

CHAPTER XVIII

MAYHEW'S VOICE had a saw's edge in it. "Now just what," he said grimly, "was the big idea behind all that?"

Monica didn't answer. She was looking at the gun as though she expected it to move of its own accord. One corner of her mouth trembled and then was still.

"Whom were you going to use it on?" he demanded.

She stirred then. "Myself," she said.

Mayhew grinned. "It looked to me as though you were counting the bullets in it when I came in. Wouldn't one be enough?"

"I don't know. I scarcely knew what I was doing. Perhaps I did look into the chamber. It was for me—you've got to believe that."

"Why?"

She moved, walked jerkily to the window, and looked out where the thick grove came near, the trees brushed with rain and the dark earth shining. "I was upset, not myself. Just—hysterical."

"You put on a good show up there by the slate pit," Mayhew said. "Finding out that your sweetheart had ulterior motives was a shock, so you covered up by pretending to faint. That gave you a chance to regain your composure."

This did not seem especially to ruffle her, but she looked at Miss Rachel standing in the door.

"Then you came back here in a hurry and ran inside to find a gun to kill yourself with. That isn't logical. You can't expect me to believe that."

"I don't care what you believe," she said evenly.

Mayhew flared: "If you think you can flout the law just because you happen to own all——"

She cut him off. "Stop it. I know what you're going to say. I own all the land in sight and I think I'm a queen. Well, for your information I don't feel that way at all. I feel like something that's crawled out of a gutter on a wet night. I wish to God I could die." She left Mayhew and went to the gun and picked it up.

Mayhew watched her sharply, but all she did was to lay the gun on her little desk. Then she made for the hall. "Excuse me, please," she said stiffly to Miss Rachel. She vanished through a near-by doorway.

Mayhew said, "I'm going to talk to that brother of hers," and he, too, left the study.

Miss Jennifer came up the hall to tell Miss Rachel that there was fresh tea in the pantry, but Miss Rachel was sitting by the window and only nodded absently at the news.

"Wouldn't you like some?" Miss Jennifer asked.

"Not just now. I'm thinking," Miss Rachel answered.

"About the murders?"

"About everything," Miss Rachel said with her eyes on the gray outline of San Cayetano.

"I'll leave you then," Miss Jennifer decided discreetly and withdrew.

It was very quiet in the little room, except for the drip of rain at the eaves. Just how many minutes ticked away during that time Miss Rachel had no way of knowing. There was a waiting quality, a malevolent patience, in the air; Miss Rachel felt her nerves rise to it like the spine hairs on a cat. But she sat still to think. It was very important, that thinking. She took her scribble of notes from her jacket pocket and reread them carefully. She hummed a scrap of tune and looked out at the rainy sky.

"How stupid we've been," she sighed at last. "We forgot the simplest rule of all: not to jump to conclusions."

Then she folded the paper and put it away and went out to look for Jennifer.

Jennifer was busy with tea, not too busy, however, to worry about Samantha and to wonder what had happened to her, shut in the tenant house alone.

"Before I sit down with you," Miss Rachel decided, "I'll run over and get her."

"You'll get wet again," Miss Jennifer worried. "Do dry out first. Or change to dry things while you're there."

Miss Rachel agreed to change and went off through the grove path to the other house. She found the kitchen cold, with remains of hers and Jennifer's scant breakfast still on the table. The hall smelled musty; the air of the upper floor touched her skin with a damp breath that she disliked. She looked through all the rooms for the cat and did not find her. Neither was there any sound of mewing in answer to her call.

For a moment Miss Rachel stood outside her bedroom door and debated whether to stop and do as Jennifer had instructed: to change to dry clothes. It would mean the advantage of discarding the several petticoats which Jennifer thought necessary and proper, since there weren't enough fresh ones to replace them. It would mean, though, the loss of several minutes. And she disliked exceedingly the chill and sluggish air of the house.

She entertained a brief wonder if someone might have come in during their absence and left some indefinable personal odor that her subconscious mind recognized and feared. But the immediate worry of what had become of Samantha drove this fugitive idea from her head. She decided to forego changing her wet things and to look for the cat outside.

She was calling Samantha at the edge of the clearing when the faintest of mewings answered her. There followed minutes of wandering back and forth to trace the sound. At last she came to the little path that led to Mr. Carder's spider hut, and she knew, not without a strange feeling around her heart, that Samantha was shut in there among Mr. Carder's collection.

The damp earth softened her footsteps, and the trees closed in behind; she had an impression of walking in utter aloneness, utter quiet. The brown door came at her suddenly, as it had before. From beyond it came the full fury of Samantha's woe.

Miss Rachel stopped and looked about her at the trees, at the turned sod, at the gray sky and the shadow of San Cayetano. Then she put a hand on the knob and pushed it. The door swung in upon darkness.

She called the cat; a medley of humiliation and woe answered her, but no black form sprang out to freedom. Dimly, then, she made out a box in the corner. Samantha was under it.

Miss Rachel stepped inside, walked the few steps to the rear of the little room, and bent over. From the corners of her eyes she could see Mr. Carder's myriad pets, plastered leggily against the glass, the green light from the skylights endowing them with a watery horror. Her skin prickled, and she rebuked herself.

"There's nothing about them," she said half aloud, lifting the box off the cat, "to be afraid of."

It was then that she heard the door close behind her with a soft click of the lock.

She spun around and ran to it and put her frail strength against its surprising firmness. She might as well have tried to move a stone. Mr. Carder had built his hut to stand. She knelt and tried to peer through the keyhole. Another eye answered her own, and a heavy breath broke into laughter. Miss Rachel drew away. Terror shook her, and the breathy laughter went on.

There was, after a while, some movement against the side of the hut. Miss Rachel listened. There were scrapings, a little thud near the eaves. It came over her suddenly that someone was getting up on the roof. She watched the skylights through a mist of spiderweb and waited.

The ladder creaked with the weight of the climber, and then a black shape swam against the sky, moved leggily over the skylight like one of Mr. Carder's pets grown giant-size. Miss Rachel, in her little prison, held her breath. She scarcely felt Samantha, still angry at her torture under the box, knead her skirt to sharpen her claws.

She saw the black shape move quickly; there was the smash of glass, and one pane of the skylight was less green. A black arm came through, a long arm, well wrapped, its hand in a heavy glove and the fingers clutching a hammer.

Miss Rachel crept along the floor to the opposite side of the narrow space and watched.

The hammer made an experimental tap against the glass pane which separated Miss Rachel from the crawling multitude on its other side, and all became clear to her. The murderer had locked her in and now meant to let loose upon her that thousand-legged horror of Mr. Carder's.

The black arm swung back through a veil of webbing. And Miss Rachel, for once in a long career of being cool and collected, screamed and tried to claw her way out through the front wall.

The hammer struck, and the glass spattered out upon the floor. Miss Rachel turned, put her back against the door, and watched as the black arm withdrew and the black shape vanished from the roof. Some torn bits of web swam through into the passage on a gust of wind. And the spiders, frightened at first by the crash of the hammer, were venturing slowly nearer the opening it had made.

Miss Rachel pulled her petticoats high, looked sickly and fearfully at the floor, and shuddered.

Mayhew had found Krug in the barn, inspecting the repairs on a tractor.

"About the barrier put up on the road to the mountain," he began without preamble. "I want to know who put it there and why."

"I ordered its erection," the grasshoppery little man said. "At Mr. Carder's suggestion. I believe there was some talk of trespassers. We have a few cattle up there, you know. Can't be too careful; thieves are always ready to make off with what's left unguarded."

Mayhew went away, found Carder in his room.

"I want to know about the barrier on the San Cayetano road. Why it was put up, when, and so on."

Carder merely looked bored, touched his white mustache idly with one finger, a book in his other hand. "Know very little about it, personally. I think Krug had something to do with it. You might ask him."

This sort of run-around gets short shrift with Mayhew. "I suggest," he said coldly, "that you join Mr. Krug, your nephews, and Miss Aldershot for a little get-together in the study. And Mr. Hale. Where might I find him?"

"I haven't the slightest," Mr. Carder answered. "Let me know when you've got them collected."

But once Mayhew had left the room Carder pushed himself out of his wheel chair and walked cautiously through the hall to the rear door. He stood for a long while looking out; he turned when Miss Jennifer put a timid hand on his arm.

"Well?" he frowned, bringing his white brows together.

"My sister is missing. She went to your tenant house a long while ago and she hasn't come back. I'm worried."

"Do you want me to go with you and look for her?"

He was still frowning; his eyes were bleak, but Miss Jennifer was too worried to notice. "I've tried to find Lieutenant Mayhew, too, but he's so busy. I suppose he's working on a clue of some kind."

"Or a dropped feather from a wild goose," Mr. Carder sneered. "But come—we'll go see about your sister."

Carder shuffled as if painfully while he was within sight of the house and then straightened up and walked as well as anyone could. He glanced at Miss Jennifer expressionlessly. "If I weren't an invalid around my nephews and my niece they'd work me to death," he said. "This is simply a matter of protective coloring." There was the brief suggestion of a grin, and then his eyes were still. "Ah, here's the path to the spider hut. She wouldn't have gone there, would she?"

Miss Jennifer timidly studied the cruel line of his mouth and decided that he wanted to have fun with her. She was beginning to regret having spoken to him in the first place. "I don't believe she'd be in there. We'd better go on."

They went through the tenant house from attic to kitchen. Mr. Carder made sly remarks about corpses, and Miss Jennifer got progressively whiter.

At the kitchen door she stopped and looked at the surrounding trees. "She came after Samantha. It wouldn't be like the cat to run away, but still——"

"There's still the spider hut," Mr. Carder offered.

Miss Jennifer wavered on the step. "I scarcely know what to do. If I could have seen Lieutenant Mayhew——"

Mr. Carder suddenly and purposefully took her arm. "We can't go back to him without having first exhausted every chance that she's still around somewhere. Now, my spider hut isn't far and it's convenient. She might have ducked in there for some reason or other. Come, we'll go see."

Miss Jennifer trembled under his touch, but she went with him. They turned from the main pathway into the little trail between the trees, and it was suddenly more silent and more damp. A branch touched Miss Jennifer's sleeve and starred it with drops of water. She was still brushing them away when the door loomed up before her.

She glanced at Mr. Carder and found him staring at the lock. "I don't hear anything," she said. "If Rachel were in there——"

"I'm quite sure that Rachel is in there." He gripped the locked door and shook it. "Someone is playing my little joke, trying to frighten her with the spiders." He rapped sharply. "Miss Murdock. Are you inside?"

A querulous mewing answered. Miss Jennifer clasped her

hands in sudden agitation. "It's Samantha! Oh, do open the door quickly! Hurry!" She put her mouth against the crack. *"Rachel!"*

He had taken out a ring of keys and was staring at them. "The key to the hut is missing. Hmmmm. . . . However, this one fits with a bit of work." He pushed Miss Jennifer aside and angled the key into the lock, lifted the knob, and strained hard. The lock clicked softly and the door opened.

The dim light gave little to see by. There was some white stuff swimming in space at about the level of Miss Jennifer's eyes. Samantha was on the sill, but she was looking backward, over her shoulder.

There was a bundle, too, a heap of something in the corner. Miss Jennifer went in to investigate. She found Rachel huddled on the box with her eyes shut. She had taken one of Rachel's hands in hers when Mr. Carder's step came, very softly, behind her.

CHAPTER XIX

MISS JENNIFER swung around in alarm, but she found Mr. Carder looking angrily at the hole in the pane into which had been stuffed—to Miss Jennifer's embarrassment—all of Rachel's starched petticoats.

Miss Rachel provided distraction then by opening one eye and sneezing.

"Rachel, you aren't dead? You're all right?" Miss Jennifer dropped to her knees, the better to clutch her sister.

Rachel stirred gingerly. "I'm frozen without those petticoats. I'm stiff and so sleepy I can hardly keep my eyes open. But I'm alive. No thanks to the visitor on the roof."

Mr. Carder stared through the torn web at the skylight. "So that's how it was done, eh? Black widows in that bunch too. You'd have been in a coma by now if one had gotten to you. Clever use of a petticoat."

"Thank you," Miss Rachel said briefly, rubbing her cramped legs through her skirt. "There are three petticoats in that collection. It's Jennifer's old-fashioned idea of what a lady ought to wear."

This public discussion of underthings so embarrassed Miss

Jennifer that she blushed. "Really, Rachel. Some things are spoken of and some aren't."

"My petticoats," Miss Rachel decided, "are now public property. They've entered criminal practice. They'll probably turn out to be Exhibit X."

Miss Jennifer subsided into a disapproving silence.

"Did you see who it was on the roof?" Mr. Carder asked.

"I'm afraid that I shall have to save all of my information for Lieutenant Mayhew," Miss Rachel told him. "He wouldn't like it otherwise. Come, Jennifer." She led the way to the door. "Don't worry about your collection, Mr. Carder. I can assure you that not a one of your unpleasant pets escaped."

Mr. Carder took out his resentment at this remark by banging the door heartily before locking it. He followed them through the grove path to the Aldershot house. Samantha persisted in looking back at him over Miss Rachel's shoulder and tried to sharpen her already sharp claws in the thin taffeta.

"He's such an unpleasant man," Miss Jennifer whispered. "He took such delight in talking about corpses in the tenant house. Do you think that he's the murderer, Rachel?"

Miss Rachel took a fugitive peep backward at Mr. Carder. "Before I can answer that question, Jennifer, there is a little experiment that I wish Lieutenant Mayhew to perform for me. Afterward—well, I believe we'll know about Mr. Carder."

The peacocks greeted them with squawkings of alarm in the courtyard. Inside Mayhew was gathered with Monica, Robert, and Harley in the study. Mr. Krug and Tommy Hale were in the hall. Mr. Krug was frightened and Tommy scornful, staring about at the rich furnishings with a carefully displayed superiority. Monica kept looking at him with a mixture of love and fear. The whole group, Miss Rachel saw, was quite nervy and upset.

Mayhew frowned at her. "Where on earth have you been keeping yourself? I've been looking for you for hours."

"But not well enough," Miss Rachel said. "I was locked in Mr. Carder's spider hut. I couldn't get out without help."

Mayhew's face grew still, his eyes watchful. "Go on. Tell me about it."

Miss Rachel sat down with the cat on a leather-covered seat flanked by a radio and a miniature bookcase. "It's quite a long story, Lieutenant. To begin with, I left here to get my cat, Samantha." She smoothed one of Samantha's ears and was rewarded by a purr. "Samantha had been left locked in the tenant house all morning. I thought she should be taken for a walk."

Miss Jennifer blushed for the second time that day.

"When I arrived at the tenant house I found no cat but an impression that someone had been in the house just previously. Perhaps our subconscious recognizes personal odors without our realizing it. However, that's mere theory." Mayhew's sigh at getting away from Miss Rachel's theories was audible. "I searched for Samantha in the house and then went outside. Eventually," Miss Rachel continued, "I heard her cries coming from Mr. Carder's spider hut. I let myself in and had bent down to let her out from under a box in the corner, when the door was shut behind me. And locked."

Mayhew's gaze stole from Krug and Tommy to Monica and her brothers; something in his look promised unfortunate consequences for the one among them who had used Miss Rachel so.

"An attempt to frighten you?" he suggested.

"Much more," Miss Rachel answered, "since there were poisonous spiders in Mr. Carder's collection, and this murderer had figured out a way to let them loose upon me."

Mayhew's still gaze fastened on her. "Did you recognize this person?"

"I'm coming to that. First I'd like to explain the murderer's method. He used a ladder to climb up on the roof of the hut, broke a pane of the skylight, reached through into the spider collection with a hammer, and broke a hole in the pane which separates the spiders from the center section."

Miss Jennifer put out a cautioning hand. "Rachel, please don't mention what you did."

"It's far too important to withhold," Miss Rachel answered. "You see, Jennifer forces me to wear a great many petticoats because she thinks that it is modest and proper. I used my petticoats to stuff up the hole the murderer had made. First, though—and while the murderer had his hand down inside that nest of spiders, before it was withdrawn—I did something which will mark him, whoever he is."

More than Mayhew were still and watchful now. The ring of faces stared at her, and for a moment her heart failed her and she thought that she could not go on. It was such a bald lie; the murderer was far too clever to be taken in by it; better to keep still. . . .

She heard her own voice saying: "I put Samantha very quickly through the opening in the glass, and she scratched the murderer on the wrist."

There was a moment of such stark, electric silence that her ears sang with it—and then, involuntarily, Robert Aldershot had turned his right hand over and was staring at the flesh below his cuff line.

He raised a white face and found all eyes on him, and a slow, purpling congestion spread upward from his collar. He stared at Miss Rachel, doubling his fist. "Why, you little——"

Mayhew burst out with: "But it was Aldershot that Tim Woodley tried to see!"

"It was Robert Aldershot whom Tim Woodley *saw,*" Miss Rachel corrected gently. "We jumped to an unwarranted conclusion there in thinking that Woodley's interview with Robert hadn't taken place. It had, of course. And Mr. Aldershot had put Woodley off on some pretext until he could get rid of him permanently. . . ."

She tried to finish speaking before it happened to her and could not. Mayhew, Tommy—none of them was quick enough to stop the ferile spring of Robert's body, the hard blow that came at her like the hammer Robert had held not so long before.

She tried to say: "Woodley, you see, was the patient sort who couldn't believe that Robert knew about Tommy's oil and wouldn't tell Tommy about it. He accepted Robert's excuses and hung around till the bitter end—his own bitter end. And I should have known that; I should have remembered Woodley's dejected appearance that last morning, his obvious disappointment in contrast to the hopeful manner he'd worn up until that time——"

But Robert's big knuckles, white, taut with his anger, came at her, bulging out of space like the approach of a cannon ball. She tried to duck, to dodge; she heard Samantha's cry of rage and a hoarse curse from Robert Aldershot.

She heard Mayhew's big feet pound the floor—and then nothing. . . .

Miss Rachel opened her eyes experimentally and then shut them again very quickly. There was an ice bag on her head, but it didn't stop the hammering pain at the back of her skull; nor did it kill the sick feeling she had that she had failed, that the murderer had felled her and escaped.

Then she glimpsed, waveringly through a fog of giddiness, Robert Aldershot, hunched on the opposite side of the study with his wrists in Mayhew's handcuffs. His eyes, set deep in their circles of dark flesh, regarded her with ferocity. There was a blue bruise on his forehead and a bleeding gash at the side of his mouth.

Mayhew, too, showed signs of considerable struggle. He bent over Miss Rachel where she lay on Monica's little sofa and patted her hand with an awkward tenderness.

She tried, to apologize; she knew how Mayhew wanted his cases tight, tidy, inevitable. "Such a silly trick. Couldn't think of another way. I knew who it was, but I couldn't prove it. . . ."

Mayhew had in his pocket a report just handed him concerning certain latent fingerprints discovered on the flesh of Tim Woodley's wrists. The prints were Robert Aldershot's, made undoubtedly when he had dragged Woodley from the car to murder him. But Mayhew didn't mention his report. He patted Miss Rachel's hand again.

"You did as well or better than I could have done. It was a good trick. It cracked the case. That's what we wanted."

Miss Rachel looked up dreamily to murmur: "I was so slow to grasp anything. Even the first clue, and a very valuable one, almost escaped me. The picture, you know; the one he himself had painted. Who but a man with his mind on murder would have left behind him the thing that represented his victory? He'd lain in that upper room so long and looked at his mountain—secure, he thought, in knowing its secret—that hearing poor, innocent Woodley babble forth the truth about it must have maddened him almost past endurance."

The cavernous eyes twitched briefly. "Woodley was such a damned fool," Robert Aldershot said. "I offered him a generous price to keep his mouth shut. It was a mistake. He refused. I had to kill him, of course."

Miss Rachel saw now what she had missed before: that Robert Aldershot's egotism justified him in everything he had done.

Mayhew said, "He admitted, while you were unconscious, that he slipped out and talked with Woodley that last night. Woodley had a fatherly interest in young Tommy, but a mistaken loyalty to his former employer made Woodley tell Robert the news first. He was angry and amazed at discovering that Robert already knew of the oil—a fact which Robert inadvertently let slip—and only Robert's promise to think over an idea for backing Tommy's development kept Woodley waiting in Los Angeles."

"And Woodley's avoidance of Florence while he was there?"

Robert Aldershot twisted his manacled wrists and grinned. He seemed to take a sudden, ironic pleasure in explaining this. "Believe it or not, it was Florence whom Woodley suspected of knowing about the oil. She had pestered young Hale to make love to her, and Woodley thought he had stumbled onto the real reason for this. He didn't know Florence's delicate methods, of course, in getting her man—whichever man had currently caught her fancy."

Miss Rachel raised her aching head. "And the map Woodley had? Did he bring a copy to you?"

"He did." The ferocity in Robert's eyes was giving way to a crazy overabundance of humor. "I made a copy before destroying it, though, and in a dumb moment I drew in a boundary that would have fixed things up perfectly if it had been the real one."

"I think," Miss Rachel considered, "that that map with its wishful-thinking boundary line was what put Florence on the right track. Wasn't it? Didn't she take it from your things and keep it, in spite of threats from you to take it away?"

Monica was weeping on Tommy's shoulder in another corner. Now she raised her head to look at her brother. "You—you even sent me looking for her. Pretending that your love for her was driving you crazy! Pretending to think that she was involved with Tommy!"

Robert shrugged. The peculiar look of humor remained. "I used such tools as came to hand. Through my uncle I had Krug instructed to look for her. . . . " A brief flash of scorn came into his face as he regarded Krug in the doorway. "The fool thought he'd driven her to suicide, came sniveling here after he'd found her body in the attic, and said we'd hounded her into killing herself. I had a hard time keeping him shut up until the body was examined by the police and the fact of murder proved." There was a certain pride in Robert's voice. He might have been talking about the completion of some difficult financial deal.

"But Florence wouldn't have betrayed you!" Tommy said grimly. "She was as cheap, as mercenary as they come. You could have bought her off."

"Her price was far too high. I tried at first to keep her satisfied with the idea of simply being my wife——"

"That song," Miss Rachel whispered. "'I Can't Give You Anything but Love, Baby.'" Miss Jennifer nodded in understanding. "I didn't realize until this afternoon what it might mean—Robert's love as a substitute for the blackmail she was trying to get out of him."

"She wouldn't have just marriage," Robert went on, the humor fading and an expression of murderous rage taking its place. "She wasn't going to be what she called a dope. She was going to have what was coming to her. She had it."

A peculiar, flitting expression of pain and surprise seemed to distract him. Then he continued: "She was waiting for me in the attic, where I had told her to be. I handed her a fat roll of bills, and while she was counting them by the candlelight I stepped behind her with Krug's razor. While she was dying I told her, very quietly, the whole story—how my father had discovered the oil seepage at the time of Hale's death in the pit—an accidental death, by the way. How my father had kept the secret, confiding it only to me, so that the knowledge of what was waiting for us would be kept from young Hale; how I had had her father fired because I was afraid he had begun to take too much interest in San Cayetano."

Monica drew a long breath. "And to think that I wanted to die because I had begun to suspect you were guilty!"

He drew back his lip. "Awkward, your pretending to faint up there. I saw that you had guessed my motive. If I had had a little more time——" He shrugged; the brief look of pain came again. "Time—never had enough—haven't much left now. You'll never hang me, you know," he cackled at Mayhew and slid sidewise on the couch. "I'm going to die on you. Maybe not right now. But soon."

Mayhew bent over him and straightened the contorted body. Robert Aldershot was blue, hollow-eyed, grinning.

Miss Rachel shut her eyes and felt tiredness sweep over her.

CHAPTER XX

MONICA STOOD outside in the dark while Mayhew carried their bags from the tenant house to his car. She seemed to be getting up her courage about something, Miss Rachel thought, and in order to make things easier Miss Rachel pretended that Samantha wanted to run away and let Monica help her put the cat into her basket.

"I'm sorry," Monica managed to say, "if I've seemed unfriendly or suspicious. Robert pretended that you had come here to spy on him and that you were part of a gang, or something. I didn't more than half believe the gang part; I just thought you were nosy and impertinent, and I'm afraid I wasn't always as decent as I might have been."

Miss Rachel, seeing Tommy waiting in the shadows of the pathway, made her answer brief. "I'm sure you've been under great difficulties and have done the best you could. Tell me, though—why did Robert permit us to come here to the tenant house?"

"He didn't know. I didn't ask him," Monica admitted. "I just—well, you see, I did sort of like you"—she touched Miss Rachel's hand softly in the dark—"and I humored you in coming here. He was furious when he knew. I couldn't understand why."

"He took his time about deciding to get rid of me," Miss Rachel said thoughtfully. "I wonder why?"

"I think that in the end his fear got the better of him," Monica answered. "There's no doubt but that he meant to kill all of us eventually. Murder must be like the rolling of a rock downhill; it gathers rubble and impetus as it goes."

"You aren't much like your brother, you know."

Monica was silent a moment. In the reflected light from Mayhew's car she looked weary and distressed. "Thank you," she said at last. "Robert was always different from the rest of us. Father tried to drill a family solidarity into us—he said it was the only way that wealth could survive—but Robert wasn't much interested. He usually took care of just himself. And he resented what Harley and I had too."

"Do you think that he really loved Florence?" Miss Rachel wondered.

"Somehow, I do. If she'd have strung along with him in getting the rest of us out of the way I believe he'd have remained married to her. It was Florence's mistake that she tried to get too much for what she knew."

Tommy's figure made a long shadow against the gloom of the trees. Far away a night bird called with a low *churring* note. The breath of orange blossoms blew with the wind from San Cayetano.

Miss Rachel put out a hand to touch Monica's arm. "Just one more thing, my dear. I don't mean to be dictatorial, but you'd better take that gold leaf off the ceiling of your bedroom. For the sake of Tommy. He has an independent spirit—I like that in a man—and I have a hunch that the gold leaf might be a fly in the ointment, to make a terribly mixed metaphor."

Monica said simply: "We're going away." Her eyes strayed to

the vast dark bulk of San Cayetano against the sky. "I'm tired of living in shadows—even golden ones."

With a last smile she had gone, and Tommy swung out to join her, and they walked off through the grove path. Miss Rachel looked after them wistfully. "What violent quarrels they're going to have," she said softly, "and what splendid reconciliations!"

Miss Jennifer came out with their handbags; Mayhew started the motor; there was an air of going away, of final and irrevocable good-by.

Miss Rachel, touched with some strange half regret, in her turn looked at the mountain sometimes called Bear Heaven.

"Come on," called Miss Jennifer. "It's getting late and we've a long drive to go."

"I know." The heights of San Cayetano were dim under the thin starshine; the last of the heavy clouds lay on the summits like the rear guard of a retreating army. Miss Rachel tried to imagine oil wells up there twinkling with lights, tried to picture San Cayetano's tall meadows laced with pipes and pitted with oil sumps; she thought of the hurrying traffic soon to be on the climbing road and the men with heavy boots who would trample San Cayetano's spring verdure.

She was glad, suddenly, to be going away.

"What are you doing, Rachel?" cried Miss Jennifer, exasperated.

The windy night, the mountain with its burden of clouds seemed to bend over her in mystery and sadness. Miss Rachel drew her jacket tight. She picked up Samantha's basket and turned her face once more toward that bulk of dark in darkness.

"I'm taking a last look—at a legend," she said.

There was then, she thought, a breath among the groves like the long sigh of a giant.

DISCUSSION QUESTIONS

- Did any aspects of the plot date the story? If so, which?

- Would the story be different if it were set in the present day? If so, how?

- Did the social context of the time play a role in the narrative? If so, how?

- If you were one of the main characters, would you have acted differently at any point in the story?

- Did you identify with any of the characters? If so, which?

- What skills or qualities make Rachel Murdock such an effective sleuth?

- Did this book remind you of any present day authors? If so, which?

MORE DOLORES HITCHENS FROM
═══ AMERICAN MYSTERY CLASSICS ═══

All titles are available in hardcover and in trade paperback.

Order from your favorite bookstore or from
The Mysterious Bookshop, 58 Warren Street, New York, N.Y. 10007
(www.mysteriousbookshop.com).

Charlotte Armstrong, *The Chocolate Cobweb*. When Amanda Garth was born, a mix-up caused the hospital to briefly hand her over to the prestigious Garrison family instead of to her birth parents. The error was quickly fixed, Amanda was never told, and the secret was forgotten for twenty-three years ... until her aunt revealed it in casual conversation. But what if the initial switch never actually occurred? **Introduction by A. J. Finn.**

Charlotte Armstrong, *The Unsuspected*. First published in 1946, this suspenseful novel opens with a young woman who has ostensibly hanged herself, leaving a suicide note. Her friend doesn't believe it and begins an investigation that puts her own life in jeopardy. It was filmed in 1947 by Warner Brothers, starring Claude Rains and Joan Caulfield. **Introduction by Otto Penzler.**

Anthony Boucher, *The Case of the Baker Street Irregulars*. When a studio announces a new hard-boiled Sherlock Holmes film, the Baker Street Irregulars begin a campaign to discredit it. Attempting to mollify them, the producers invite members to the set, where threats are received, each referring to one of the original Holmes tales, followed by murder. Fortunately, the amateur sleuths use Holmesian lessons to solve the crime. **Introduction by Otto Penzler.**

Anthony Boucher, *Rocket to the Morgue*. Hilary Foulkes has made so many enemies that it is difficult to speculate who was responsible for stabbing him nearly to death in a room with only one door through which no one was seen entering or leaving. This classic locked room mystery is populated by such thinly disguised science fiction legends as Robert Heinlein, L. Ron Hubbard, and John W. Campbell. **Introduction by F. Paul Wilson.**

Fredric Brown, *The Fabulous Clipjoint*. Brown's outstanding mystery won an Edgar as the best first novel of the year (1947). When Wallace Hunter is found dead in an alley after a long night of drinking, the police don't really care. But his teenage son Ed and his uncle Am, the carnival worker, are convinced that some things don't add up and the crime isn't what it seems to be. **Introduction by Lawrence Block.**

John Dickson Carr, *The Crooked Hinge*. Selected by a group of mystery experts as one of the 15 best impossible crime novels ever written, this is one of Gideon Fell's greatest challenges. Estranged from his family for 25 years, Sir John Farnleigh returns to England from America to claim his inheritance but another person turns up claiming that he can prove he is the real Sir John. Inevitably, one of them is murdered. **Introduction by Charles Todd.**

John Dickson Carr, *The Eight of Swords*. When Gideon Fell arrives at a crime scene, it appears to be straightforward enough. A man has been shot to death in an unlocked room and the likely perpetrator was a recent visitor. But Fell discovers inconsistencies and his investigations are complicated by an apparent poltergeist, some American gangsters, and two meddling amateur sleuths. **Introduction by Otto Penzler.**

John Dickson Carr, *The Mad Hatter Mystery*. A prankster has been stealing top hats all around London. Gideon Fell suspects that the same person may be responsible for the theft of a manuscript of a long-lost story by Edgar Allan Poe. The hats reappear in unexpected but conspicuous places but, when one is found on the head of a corpse by the Tower of London, it is evident that the thefts are more than pranks. **Introduction by Otto Penzler.**

John Dickson Carr, *The Plague Court Murders*. When murder occurs in a locked hut on Plague Court, an estate haunted by the ghost of a hangman's assistant who died a victim of the black death, Sir Henry Merrivale seeks a logical solution to a ghostly crime. A spiritual medium employed to rid the house of his spirit is found stabbed to death in a locked stone hut on the grounds, surrounded by an untouched circle of mud. **Introduction by Michael Dirda.**

John Dickson Carr, *The Red Widow Murders*. In a "haunted" mansion, the room known as the Red Widow's Chamber proves lethal to all who spend the night. Eight people investigate and the one who draws the ace of spades must sleep in it. The room is locked from the inside and watched all night by the others. When the door is unlocked, the victim has been poisoned. Enter Sir Henry Merrivale to solve the crime. **Introduction by Tom Mead.**

Frances Crane, *The Turquoise Shop*. In an arty little New Mexico town, Mona Brandon has arrived from the East and becomes the subject of gossip about her money, her influence, and the corpse in the nearby desert who may be her husband. Pat Holly, who runs the local gift shop, is as interested as anyone in the goings on—but even more in Pat Abbott, the detective investigating the possible murder. **Introduction by Anne Hillerman.**

Todd Downing, *Vultures in the Sky*. There is no end to the series of terrifying events that befall a luxury train bound for Mexico. First, a man dies when the train passes through a dark tunnel, then it comes to an abrupt stop in the middle of the desert. More deaths occur when night falls and the passengers panic when they realize they are trapped with a murderer on the loose. **Introduction by James Sallis.**

Mignon G. Eberhart, *Murder by an Aristocrat*. Nurse Keate is called to help a man who has been "accidentally" shot in the shoulder. When he is murdered while convalescing, it is clear that there was no accident. Although a killer is loose in the mansion, the family seems more concerned that news of the murder will leave their circle. *The New Yorker* wrote than "Eberhart can weave an almost flawless mystery." **Introduction by Nancy Pickard.**

Erle Stanley Gardner, *The Case of the Baited Hook*. Perry Mason gets a phone call in the middle of the night and his potential client says it's urgent, that he has two one-thousand-dollar bills that he will give him as a retainer, with an additional ten-thousand whenever he is called on to represent him. When

Mason takes the case, it is not for the caller but for a beautiful woman whose identity is hidden behind a mask. **Introduction by Otto Penzler.**

Erle Stanley Gardner, *The Case of the Borrowed Brunette*. A mysterious man named Mr. Hines has advertised a job for a woman who has to fulfill very specific physical requirements. Eva Martell, pretty but struggling in her career as a model, takes the job but her aunt smells a rat and hires Perry Mason to investigate. Her fears are realized when Hines turns up in the apartment with a bullet hole in his head. **Introduction by Otto Penzler.**

Erle Stanley Gardner, *The Case of the Careless Kitten*. Helen Kendal receives a mysterious phone call from her vanished uncle Franklin, long presumed dead, who urges her to contact Perry Mason. Soon, she finds herself the main suspect in the murder of an unfamiliar man. Her kitten has just survived a poisoning attempt—as has her aunt Matilda. What is the connection between Franklin's return and the murder attempts? **Introduction by Otto Penzler.**

Erle Stanley Gardner, *The Case of the Rolling Bones*. One of Gardner's most successful Perry Mason novels opens with a clear case of blackmail, though the person being blackmailed claims he isn't. It is not long before the police are searching for someone wanted for killing the same man in two different states—thirty-three years apart. The confounding puzzle of what happened to the dead man's toes is a challenge. **Introduction by Otto Penzler.**

Erle Stanley Gardner, *The Case of the Shoplifter's Shoe*. Most cases for Perry Mason involve murder but here he is hired because a young woman fears her aunt is a kleptomaniac. Sarah may not have been precisely the best guardian for a collection of valuable diamonds and, sure enough, they go missing. When the jeweler is found shot dead, Sarah is spotted leaving the murder scene with a bundle of gems stuffed in her purse. **Introduction by Otto Penzler.**

Erle Stanley Gardner, *The Bigger They Come*. Gardner's first novel using the pseudonym A.A. Fair starts off a series featuring the large and loud Bertha Cool and her employee, the small and meek Donald Lam. Given the job of delivering divorce papers to an evident crook,

Lam can't find him—but neither can the police. The *Los Angeles Times* called this book: "Breathlessly dramatic … an original." Introduction by Otto Penzler.

Frances Noyes Hart, *The Bellamy Trial.* Inspired by the real-life Hall-Mills case, the most sensational trial of its day, this is the story of Stephen Bellamy and Susan Ives, accused of murdering Bellamy's wife Madeleine. Eight days of dynamic testimony, some true, some not, make headlines for an enthralled public. Rex Stout called this historic courtroom thriller one of the ten best mysteries of all time. Introduction by Hank Phillippi Ryan.

H.F. Heard, *A Taste for Honey.* The elderly Mr. Mycroft quietly keeps bees in Sussex, where he is approached by the reclusive and somewhat misanthropic Mr. Silchester, whose honey supplier was found dead, stung to death by her bees. Mycroft, who shares many traits with Sherlock Holmes, sets out to find the vicious killer. Rex Stout described it as "sinister … a tale well and truly told." Introduction by Otto Penzler.

Dolores Hitchens, *The Alarm of the Black Cat.* Detective fiction aficionado Rachel Murdock has a peculiar meeting with a little girl and a dead toad, sparking her curiosity about a love triangle that has sparked anger. When the girl's great grandmother is found dead, Rachel and her cat Samantha work with a friend in the Los Angeles Police Department to get to the bottom of things. Introduction by David Handler.

Dolores Hitchens, *The Cat Saw Murder.* Miss Rachel Murdock, the highly intelligent 70-year-old amateur sleuth, is not entirely heartbroken when her slovenly, unattractive, bridge-cheating niece is murdered. Miss Rachel is happy to help the socially maladroit and somewhat bumbling Detective Lieutenant Stephen Mayhew, retaining her composure when a second brutal murder occurs. Introduction by Joyce Carol Oates.

Dorothy B. Hughes, *Dread Journey.* A bigshot Hollywood producer has worked on his magnum opus for years, hiring and firing one beautiful starlet after another. But Kitten Agnew's contract won't allow her to be fired, so she fears she might be terminated more permanently. Together with the producer on a train journey from Hollywood to Chicago, Kitten becomes more terrified with each passing mile. Introduction by Sarah Weinman.

Dorothy B. Hughes, *Ride the Pink Horse.* When Sailor met Willis Douglass, he was just a poor kid who Douglass groomed to work as a confidential secretary. As the senator became increasingly corrupt, he knew he could count on Sailor to clean up his messes. No longer a senator, Douglass flees Chicago for Santa Fe, leaving behind a murder rap and Sailor as the prime suspect. Seeking vengeance, Sailor follows. Introduction by Sara Paretsky.

Dorothy B. Hughes, *The So Blue Marble.* Set in the glamorous world of New York high society, this novel became a suspense classic as twins from Europe try to steal a rare and beautiful gem owned by an aristocrat whose sister is an even more menacing presence. *The New Yorker* called it "Extraordinary … [Hughes'] brilliant descriptive powers make and unmake reality." Introduction by Otto Penzler.

W. Bolingbroke Johnson, *The Widening Stain.* After a cocktail party, the attractive Lucie Coindreau, a "black-eyed, black-haired Frenchwoman" visits the rare books wing of the library and apparently takes a headfirst fall from an upper gallery. Dismissed as a horrible accident, it seems dubious when Professor Hyett is strangled while reading a priceless 12th-century manuscript, which has gone missing. Introduction by Nicholas A. Basbanes

Baynard Kendrick, *Blind Man's Bluff.* Blinded in World War II, Duncan Maclain forms a successful private detective agency, aided by his two dogs. Here, he is called on to solve the case of a blind man who plummets from the top of an eight-story building, apparently with no one present except his dead-drunk son. Introduction by Otto Penzler.

Baynard Kendrick, *The Odor of Violets.* Duncan Maclain, a blind former intelligence officer, is asked to investigate the murder of an actor in his Greenwich Village apartment. This would cause a stir at any time but, when the actor possesses secret government plans that then go missing, it's enough to interest the local police as well as the American government and Maclain, who suspects a German spy plot. Introduction by Otto Penzler.

C. Daly King, *Obelists at Sea*. On a cruise ship traveling from New York to Paris, the lights of the smoking room briefly go out, a gunshot crashes through the night, and a man is dead. Two detectives are on board but so are four psychiatrists who believe their professional knowledge can solve the case by understanding the psyche of the killer—each with a different theory. **Introduction by Martin Edwards.**

Jonathan Latimer, *Headed for a Hearse*. Featuring Bill Crane, the booze-soaked Chicago private detective, this humorous hard-boiled novel was filmed as *The Westland Case* in 1937 starring Preston Foster. Robert Westland has been framed for the grisly murder of his wife in a room with doors and windows locked from the inside. As the day of his execution nears, he relies on Crane to find the real murderer. **Introduction by Max Allan Collins**

Lange Lewis, *The Birthday Murder*. Victoria is a successful novelist and screenwriter and her husband is a movie director so their marriage seems almost too good to be true. Then, on her birthday, her happy new life comes crashing down when her husband is murdered using a method of poisoning that was described in one of her books. She quickly becomes the leading suspect. **Introduction by Randal S. Brandt.**

Frances and Richard Lockridge, *Death on the Aisle*. In one of the most beloved books to feature Mr. and Mrs. North, the body of a wealthy backer of a play is found dead in a seat of the 45th Street Theater. Pam is thrilled to engage in her favorite pastime—playing amateur sleuth—much to the annoyance of Jerry, her publisher husband. The Norths inspired a stage play, a film, and long-running radio and TV series. **Introduction by Otto Penzler.**

John P. Marquand, *Your Turn, Mr. Moto*. The first novel about Mr. Moto, originally titled *No Hero*, is the story of a World War I hero pilot who finds himself jobless during the Depression. In Tokyo for a big opportunity that falls apart, he meets a Japanese agent and his Russian colleague and the pilot suddenly finds himself caught in a web of intrigue. Peter Lorre played Mr. Moto in a series of popular films. **Introduction by Lawrence Block.**

Stuart Palmer, *The Penguin Pool Murder*. The first adventure of schoolteacher and dedicated amateur sleuth Hildegarde Withers occurs at the New York Aquarium when she and her young students notice a corpse in one of the tanks. It was published in 1931 and filmed the next year, starring Edna May Oliver as the American Miss Marple—though much funnier than her English counterpart. **Introduction by Otto Penzler.**

Stuart Palmer, *The Puzzle of the Happy Hooligan*. New York City schoolteacher Hildegarde Withers cannot resist "assisting" homicide detective Oliver Piper. In this novel, she is on vacation in Hollywood and on the set of a movie about Lizzie Borden when the screenwriter is found dead. Six comic films about Withers appeared in the 1930s, most successfully starring Edna May Oliver. **Introduction by Otto Penzler.**

Otto Penzler, ed., *Golden Age Bibliomysteries*. Stories of murder, theft, and suspense occur with alarming regularity in the unlikely world of books and bibliophiles, including bookshops, libraries, and private rare book collections, written by such giants of the mystery genre as Ellery Queen, Cornell Woolrich, Lawrence G. Blochman, Vincent Starrett, and Anthony Boucher. **Introduction by Otto Penzler.**

Otto Penzler, ed., *Golden Age Detective Stories*. The history of American mystery fiction has its pantheon of authors who have influenced and entertained readers for nearly a century, reaching its peak during the Golden Age, and this collection pays homage to the work of the most acclaimed: Cornell Woolrich, Erle Stanley Gardner, Craig Rice, Ellery Queen, Dorothy B. Hughes, Mary Roberts Rinehart, and more. **Introduction by Otto Penzler.**

Otto Penzler, ed., *Golden Age Locked Room Mysteries*. The so-called impossible crime category reached its zenith during the 1920s, 1930s, and 1940s, and this volume includes the greatest of the great authors who mastered the form: John Dickson Carr, Ellery Queen, C. Daly King, Clayton Rawson, and Erle Stanley Gardner. Like great magicians, these literary conjurors will baffle and delight readers. **Introduction by Otto Penzler.**

Ellery Queen, *The Adventures of Ellery Queen*. These stories are the earliest short works to feature Queen as a detective and are among the best of the author's fair-play mysteries. So many of the elements that comprise the gestalt of Queen may be found in these tales: alternate solutions, the dying clue, a bizarre crime, and the author's ability to find fresh variations of works by other authors. **Introduction by Otto Penzler.**

Ellery Queen, *The American Gun Mystery*. A rodeo comes to New York City at the Colosseum. The headliner is Buck Horne, the once popular film cowboy who opens the show leading a charge of forty whooping cowboys until they pull out their guns and fire into the air. Buck falls to the ground, shot dead. The police instantly lock the doors to search everyone but the offending weapon has completely vanished. **Introduction by Otto Penzler.**

Ellery Queen, *The Chinese Orange Mystery*. The offices of publisher Donald Kirk have seen strange events but nothing like this. A strange man is found dead with two long spears alongside his back. And, though no one was seen entering or leaving the room, everything has been turned backwards or upside down: pictures face the wall, the victim's clothes are worn backwards, the rug upside down. Why in the world? **Introduction by Otto Penzler.**

Ellery Queen, *The Dutch Shoe Mystery*. Millionaire philanthropist Abagail Doorn falls into a coma and she is rushed to the hospital she funds for an emergency operation by one of the leading surgeons on the East Coast. When she is wheeled into the operating theater, the sheet covering her body is pulled back to reveal her garroted corpse—the first of a series of murders **Introduction by Otto Penzler.**

Ellery Queen, *The Egyptian Cross Mystery*. A small-town schoolteacher is found dead, headed, and tied to a T-shaped cross on December 25th, inspiring such sensational headlines as "Crucifixion on Christmas Day." Amateur sleuth Ellery Queen is so intrigued he travels to Virginia but fails to solve the crime. Then a similar murder takes place on New York's Long Island—and then another. **Introduction by Otto Penzler.**

Ellery Queen, *The Siamese Twin Mystery*. When Ellery and his father encounter a raging forest fire on a mountain, their only hope is to drive up to an isolated hillside manor owned by a secretive surgeon and his strange guests. While playing solitaire in the middle of the night, the doctor is shot. The only clue is a torn playing card. Suspects include a society beauty, a valet, and conjoined twins. **Introduction by Otto Penzler.**

Ellery Queen, *The Spanish Cape Mystery*. Amateur detective Ellery Queen arrives in the resort town of Spanish Cape soon after a young woman and her uncle are abducted by a gun-toting, one-eyed giant. The next day, the woman's somewhat dicey boyfriend is found murdered—totally naked under a black fedora and opera cloak. **Introduction by Otto Penzler.**

Patrick Quentin, *A Puzzle for Fools*. Broadway producer Peter Duluth takes to the bottle when his wife dies but enters a sanitarium to dry out. Malevolent events plague the hospital, including when Peter hears his own voice intone, "There will be murder." And there is. He investigates, aided by a young woman who is also a patient. This is the first of nine mysteries featuring Peter and Iris Duluth. **Introduction by Otto Penzler.**

Clayton Rawson, *Death from a Top Hat*. When the New York City Police Department is baffled by an apparently impossible crime, they call on The Great Merlini, a retired stage magician who now runs a Times Square magic shop. In his first case, two occultists have been murdered in a room locked from the inside, their bodies positioned to form a pentagram. **Introduction by Otto Penzler.**

Craig Rice, *Eight Faces at Three*. Gin-soaked John J. Malone, defender of the guilty, is notorious for getting his culpable clients off. It's the innocent ones who are problems. Like Holly Inglehart, accused of piercing the black heart of her well-heeled aunt Alexandria with a lovely Florentine paper cutter. No one who knew the old battle-ax liked her, but Holly's prints were found on the murder weapon. **Introduction by Lisa Lutz.**

Craig Rice, *Home Sweet Homicide*. Known as the Dorothy Parker of mystery fiction for her memorable wit, Craig Rice was the first detective writer to appear on the cover of *Time* magazine. This comic mystery features two kids who are trying to find a husband for their widowed mother while she's engaged in sleuthing. Filmed with the same title in 1946 with Peggy Ann Garner and Randolph Scott. **Introduction by Otto Penzler.**

Mary Roberts Rinehart, *The Album.* Crescent Place is a quiet enclave of wealthy people in which nothing ever happens—until a bedridden old woman is attacked by an intruder with an ax. *The New York Times* stated: "All Mary Roberts Rinehart mystery stories are good, but this one is better." **Introduction by Otto Penzler.**

Mary Roberts Rinehart, *The Haunted Lady.* The arsenic in her sugar bowl was wealthy widow Eliza Fairbanks' first clue that somebody wanted her dead. Nightly visits of bats, birds, and rats, obviously aimed at scaring the dowager to death, was the second. Eliza calls the police, who send nurse Hilda Adams, the amateur sleuth they refer to as "Miss Pinkerton," to work undercover to discover the culprit. **Introduction by Otto Penzler.**

Mary Roberts Rinehart, *Miss Pinkerton.* Hilda Adams is a nurse, not a detective, but she is observant and smart and so it is common for Inspector Patton to call on her for help. Her success results in his calling her "Miss Pinkerton." *The New Republic* wrote: "From thousands of hearts and homes the cry will go up: Thank God for Mary Roberts Rinehart." **Introduction by Carolyn Hart.**

Mary Roberts Rinehart, *The Red Lamp.* Professor William Porter refuses to believe that the seaside manor he's just inherited is haunted but he has to convince his wife to move in. However, he soon sees evidence of the occult phenomena of which the townspeople speak. Whether it is a spirit or a human being, Porter accepts that there is a connection to the rash of murders that have terrorized the countryside. **Introduction by Otto Penzler.**

Mary Roberts Rinehart, *The Wall.* For two decades, Mary Roberts Rinehart was the second-best-selling author in America (only Sinclair Lewis outsold her) and was beloved for her tales of suspense. In a magnificent mansion, the ex-wife of one of the owners turns up making demands and is found dead the next day. And there are more dark secrets lying behind the walls of the estate. **Introduction by Otto Penzler.**

Joel Townsley Rogers, *The Red Right Hand.* This extraordinary whodunnit that is as puzzling as it is terrifying was identified by crime fiction scholar Jack Adrian as "one of the dozen or so finest mystery novels of the 20th century." A deranged killer sends a doctor on a quest for the truth—deep into the recesses of his own mind—when he and his bride-to-be elope but pick up a terrifying sharp-toothed hitch-hiker. **Introduction by Joe R. Lansdale.**

Roger Scarlett, *Cat's Paw.* The family of the wealthy old bachelor Martin Greenough cares far more about his money than they do about him. For his birthday, he invites all his potential heirs to his mansion to tell them what they hope to hear. Before he can disburse funds, however, he is murdered, and the Boston Police Department's big problem is that there are too many suspects. **Introduction by Curtis Evans**

Vincent Starrett, *Dead Man Inside.* 1930s Chicago is a tough town but some crimes are more bizarre than others. Customers arrive at a haberdasher to find a corpse in the window and a sign on the door: *Dead Man Inside! I am Dead. The store will not open today.* This is just one of a series of odd murders that terrorizes the city. Reluctant detective Walter Ghost leaps into action to learn what is behind the plague. **Introduction by Otto Penzler.**

Vincent Starrett, *The Great Hotel Murder.* Theater critic and amateur sleuth Riley Blackwood investigates a murder in a Chicago hotel where the dead man had changed rooms with a stranger who had registered under a fake name. *The New York Times* described it as "an ingenious plot with enough complications to keep the reader guessing." **Introduction by Lyndsay Faye.**

Vincent Starrett, *Murder on 'B' Deck.* Walter Ghost, a psychologist, scientist, explorer, and former intelligence officer, is on a cruise ship and his friend novelist Dunsten Mollock, a Nigel Bruce-like Watson whose role is to offer occasional comic relief, accommodates when he fails to leave the ship before it takes off. Although they make mistakes along the way, the amateur sleuths solve the shipboard murders. **Introduction by Ray Betzner.**

Phoebe Atwood Taylor, *The Cape Cod Mystery*. Vacationers have flocked to Cape Cod to avoid the heat wave that hit the Northeast and find their holiday unpleasant when the area is flooded with police trying to find the murderer of a muckraking journalist who took a cottage for the season. Finding a solution falls to Asey Mayo, "the Cape Cod Sherlock," known for his worldly wisdom, folksy humor, and common sense. **Introduction by Otto Penzler.**

S. S. Van Dine, *The Benson Murder Case.* The first of 12 novels to feature Philo Vance, the most popular and influential detective character of the early part of the 20th century. When wealthy stockbroker Alvin Benson is found shot to death in a locked room in his mansion, the police are baffled until the erudite flaneur and art collector arrives on the scene. Paramount filmed it in 1930 with William Powell as Vance. **Introduction by Ragnar Jónasson.**

Cornell Woolrich, *The Bride Wore Black.* The first suspense novel by one of the greatest of all noir authors opens with a bride and her new husband walking out of the church. A car speeds by, shots ring out, and he falls dead at her feet. Determined to avenge his death, she tracks down everyone in the car, concluding with a shocking surprise. It was filmed by Francois Truffaut in 1968, starring Jeanne Moreau. **Introduction by Eddie Muller.**

Cornell Woolrich, *Deadline at Dawn.* Quinn is overcome with guilt about having robbed a stranger's home. He meets Bricky, a dime-a-dance girl, and they fall for each other. When they return to the crime scene, they discover a dead body. Knowing Quinn will be accused of the crime, they race to find the true killer before he's arrested. A 1946 film starring Susan Hayward was loosely based on the plot. **Introduction by David Gordon.**

Cornell Woolrich, *Waltz into Darkness.* A New Orleans businessman successfully courts a woman through the mail but he is shocked to find when she arrives that she is not the plain brunette whose picture he'd received but a radiant blond beauty. She soon absconds with his fortune. Wracked with disappointment and loneliness, he vows to track her down. When he finds her, the real nightmare begins. **Introduction by Wallace Stroby.**